Alpha Professor

ZOE RAY

Alpha Professor by Zoe Ray

Copyright © 2020 by Zoe Ray.

All rights reserved. Published by Z Ray Publishing.

Alpha Professor is a work of fiction. Names, characters, businesses, places, events and incidents are either the products of the author's imagination or used in a fictitious manner. Any resemblance to actual persons, living or dead, or actual events is purely coincidental.

I ~ Shante

Day one, and I'm already screwing up. "Excuse me. Move. Sorry. Damnit. Come on." I roll my eyes as I pass the woman giving me a death stare while I power walk through the halls like a madwoman. I don't have time to be polite. It must be nice to stand around while I'm trying my hardest to make it to class on time. I wish I could live a life of leisure, like the other students here. I've got to make this school thing work. I've shoved at least three people because I really don't want to be late for my first day.

My plan was to be early, but I had to work late. Traffic was a nightmare, and I went into the wrong building when I got here. I have two minutes to make it to class, and I think I can do it. I frantically look at the wall in front of me. Should I go left or right to get to room number 153? Why are the numbers so small? I squint my eyes and ignore the stale stench of the dimly lit hallways. Room 153 should be on the right. I turn the corner and clutch my books while my purse flops on my arm. It's been a while since I went to school, but I'm starting to remember why people carry backpacks.

There's a girl that's been on my tail for a while. I wonder if she's going to the same class as me. I look to the left and right. Damn, it's not in this hallway. Who built this building? I'm close. It should be in the left corridor. I speed up to turn the corner, and out of nowhere, I'm knocked back. My books fall to the floor with a loud thud, and a strong pair of arms stop me from falling on the floor.

"Seriously," I yell as he steadies me. I swat the hands away and bend over to pick up my books.

"Whoa. Are you okay?" He bends over to help me. All I can see are his clothes at this point, but he's so close to me, even that's a blur.

"I'm fine. I got it," I say without looking up.

"Sorry, I didn't see you," he says.

"It's all right," I say as I rise. My purse slides down my arm, and I struggle to hold it up with my books in my hands.

"Can I carry those for you?"

"No, thank you. I have to go." I finally look up, and a handsome man is smiling down at me. He looks like trouble. I love trouble, but I don't have time for it. I have to go. Although, I wouldn't mind seeing some eye candy the next time I'm in the hallway. He's watching me. I can feel it. Why did I wear this skirt today? I'm suddenly aware my thighs have been rubbing together. The friction is becoming uncomfortable. It feels like I'm about to start a fire.

Room 153 is the only classroom on this hallway. There's a glass door at the end, a few feet from the room. The sun hasn't set yet, and daylight peeks through an otherwise dark corridor. Finally, I see it. I'm two minutes late, but everyone's probably still getting settled. I'm sure class hasn't even started yet.

Before I turn the door handle, I catch my breath. I open the door and walk in. I spot a couple of empty seats. I can't zero in on anyone's face. I'm too busy trying to figure out which chair I want to sit in. The only other thing in my head is empty noise.

"Young lady." A man's voice catches my attention.

I've zeroed in on a chair in the back of the room and head in that direction.

"Where are you going?"

I look around the room, trying to figure out who he's talking to.

"I'm talking to you," he says.

I turn around. "I'm looking for a s—"

My mouth hangs open, and I lose my train of thought when I see the man who stands in front of the room. My underarms and palms sweat. I blink to make sure he's real. "Are you the professor?" I ask.

"Yes."

"I'm loving this class already," I say. Laughter erupts throughout the room. I can't help but laugh myself. I know my cheeks are flushed, but I don't care because I can tell the professor is fighting a smile.

I've never had a teacher who looked like this before. Big, sexy, chocolate and all I want to do is lick him. He has hazel eyes, a chiseled jawline, and just enough scruff under his chin. He's wearing a white button-down shirt underneath a light blue sweater and blue slacks. I don't know whether I love or hate his preppy style. Guys don't dress like him where I'm from. I don't think I've ever met a man like him.

"You're distracting my class."

"Sorry, I was trying to find a seat," I say.

"If you were here on time, you'd know class begins at six on the dot, and no one will be allowed inside after that."

"I understand. It won't happen again."

"What's your name, Miss?"

"Shante."

He looks at the paper in his hand. "Shante Wilson."

"Yes, that's me."

"Miss Wilson, I hope it doesn't happen again, but you'll have to leave and come back on Wednesday, and you'll have to be on time."

"You can't be serious. It's two minutes. Blame the guy that knocked me over in that labyrinth of a hallway."

—

3

As I look around the room, some of the faces come into focus. Everyone is staring at me. The class is mostly women ranging from late teens to late forties and two men. I was right. The woman who was on my tail is sitting in the second row. I think that heifer is smirking. My eyes roll. This is not how I imagined my day going.

He sits on the edge of his desk. "I don't make exceptions, and the law certainly does not care about your excuses. You've already disrupted my class."

"With all due respect, you're the one disrupting class. Do you care about rules more than you care about people? Is that the message you're sending?"

"You need to leave, Miss Wilson."

"Absolutely not," I say.

People gasp.

"I wasn't asking."

"I'm not leaving. I paid for this class."

"Everyone paid for this class, and they showed up on time. Take this." He takes a stack of papers off his desk and hands them to me.

I look at the first page. It's a syllabus, **Intro to Law, Professor Jeremiah B. Johnson, JD.**

"See you on Wednesday if you can make it on time, Miss Wilson."

Professor Johnson turns his attention to the class and starts taking attendance as if I'm not standing here. I put my hand on my hip and wait.

Once he finishes, he turns his attention to me. "That'll be all, Miss Wilson."

"I can't believe this."

"Let's have a conversation in the hallway before class resumes."

I don't trust him.

He must sense this because he holds out his hand and nods. "It'll only be a minute."

His eyes draw me in. I reluctantly follow him into the hallway. He closes the door and stands inches away from me. His body towers over mine.

—

4

My neck extends as I look up at him. His presence is powerful. I inhale. I don't know what that scent is, but he smells like heaven, and I want to bury my nose in his chest. Heat radiates from his skin. The sound of my name snaps me back to reality. What is he doing to me? He's perfect, he's sexy, but he's not my type.

"Miss Wilson," he repeats.

I'm annoyed with his proper attitude. "Why are you calling me, Miss Wilson? Call me, Shante, Jeremiah."

"You'll address me as Professor Johnson. I'm appalled by your behavior, and I'd appreciate it if you'd refrain from causing a scene in my classroom. These kinds of outbursts won't be tolerated."

"Is that right, Jeremiah?"

"How old are you exactly?"

"Old enough to keep up with you, professor." I smirk.

"Excuse me."

"Relax. I'm just playing with you. I know I look young, but I'm pretty sure we're around the same age."

"Then I expect more from you. You should set a better example for the younger students."

"I ain't nobody's mama. I'm just here to get my credits."

"Look over the syllabus. The reading for the next class is listed. I need to know you're serious about this course. If not, you may as well drop this class now because I won't hesitate to fail you."

"You're too damn handsome to be so uptight, Jeremiah."

He grins. "I have to get back to class. Goodnight, Miss Wilson."

"Shante," I remind him.

"See you next class."

"You can't make me leave."

His voice deepens as he steps closer to me. His face only a few inches away from mine. "Let's get something straight. I'm capable of making you do many things, but I think you already know that, don't you, Shante."

5

My eyes are glued to his lips and his perfect white teeth. I nod in agreement as he wills my gaze to follow his eyes. "Yes," I whisper. Did he just hypnotize me? I cross my legs and squeeze as tight as I can. I don't know how Poindexter has me dripping wet.

"Yes, Professor Johnson," he says.

"Yes, Professor Johnson," I repeat.

"Good girl."

"Are you flirting with me?"

"No."

"It won't work."

"I have to get back to my class," he says. "I'll have to deal with you later."

"We have to get back to class."

He sighs with frustration. Before he can open the door, he turns to me and grabs my books.

I instinctively reach for them. "What are you doing?"

He bends his knees and uses his other arm to lift me over his shoulder. The transition is effortless. The urge to kick escapes me, because his touch feels so good. The palm of his hand rests on the back of my thigh, heating my skin. My body is begging him to slip that hand under my skirt.

I gasp. "Professor Johnson."

He walks a few feet to the door at the end of the hallway.

"Jeremiah, what are you doing?" I try to hold my skirt down so I don't flash the whole school, but as I look around there's no one here to see this. Unbelievable.

Jeremiah says nothing.

"Isn't it against the rules to pick up students?" I ask.

"It's a good thing you don't care about the rules."

He slowly slides me down the side of his body. I feel every bulge and every muscle. His arm runs over my leg, my ass, my back. Time stands still when I'm eye to eye with him. Our faces are centimeters apart. His breathing is as heavy as mine. His eyes light up, literally, with flashes of a deep golden brown, a contrast from their light, pale

—
6

color. Our mouths are so close, I can inhale his breath. I swear he's going to kiss me, and I think I'm going to let him. What am I thinking? I can't do that.

He releases his firm grip, and I regret that the moment is over. I slide the rest of the way to the floor. I'm only five foot four. He's at least a foot taller than me, maybe more.

"Give me my books," I yell.

"Here you go," he holds them out, and I grab them.

"What the hell is wrong with you?"

"Goodnight, Miss Wilson."

He closes the door with me on the other side. It's hard to believe this sophisticated man who thinks he's better than everybody else behaves this way. I yank on the door to confirm my suspicion. It's locked. I'm fuming as I watch him walk away. All this for a community college course.

I'm worn out, defeated. I spot a nearby bench in the midst of the patchy grass and take a seat. I know I'm not crazy. He overreacted to me being a few minutes late. He humiliated me. I don't even know if I want to show my face here on Wednesday. I should report him to whoever you report people to in this damn school. My elbows move to my lap and my head between my palms as I rock back and forth, fuming, frustrated, and fixated on Jeremiah B. Johnson.

I don't need this. It seems like every time I try to do anything to better myself, the world turns against me. I can't be that bad of a person.

I almost forgot what I'm doing here. I work at a law firm as a receptionist. I find answering phones and greeting people unfulfilling. They don't give me any real work to do. A paralegal position came up, and I applied. I told my boss I wanted to be challenged, and I was told I needed experience or education. I have neither. I dropped out of college what seems like a lifetime ago, and my life has lacked direction ever since. I lost track of any goals I had and only focused on getting by.

—

Now I want more. Assisting lawyers with trial stuff, shit, I can do that. I'm obsessed with Erin Brockovich, and I figure being a paralegal is close enough. Plus, she did it as a single mother. Nothing is stopping me. What would Erin Brockovich do? I wonder. She wouldn't allow an arrogant prick, like Jeremiah B. Johnson, stop her.

"He messed with the wrong one today," I say to myself.

"Excuse me. Are you okay?"

I look up and see a handsome face staring back at me. "You always seem to be around at my worst moments," I say to the man I ran into earlier in the hallway. I look at the tattoos on his arms. His body is lean but muscular. His blue jeans and black shirt along with his gold chain, bring his masculine, edgy look together. He smiles when I look at him. His golden-brown complexion and his wavy, faded haircut are everything I try to avoid in a man, along with that panty melting smile. He knows he's fine.

"Maybe I'm here to make them better," he says.

"I think I'll be okay. What are you doing out here?" I ask.

"I was walking by when I saw you sitting here. I assumed you were going to class when you knocked me over. Were you really just fleeing the building?"

"I was going to class, but I got kicked out."

"Kicked out? You're fucking with me."

I snap my head back. "No, I can't believe it either."

"Who kicked you out of class on the first day?" He sits next to me.

I shuffle my body around and slide an inch away from him. "Professor Jeremiah Johnson, JD." I say his name with disdain.

"Oh, Johnson. Do you want me to go have a talk with him? I can kick his ass."

"I don't even know you," I say, but he confirmed my suspicion. He's trouble.

"Sorry, I'm Strike."

"Strike? That's your name?"

"That's what they call me."

"Who calls you that?"

"It's what they called me in the neighborhood, growing up, you know how it is."

"No, I don't. Why do they call you Strike?"

"You only get one strike with me."

"Then, you're out?" I ask.

He laughs. "Exactly."

"I don't even want to know what that means," I say. Red flags are waving all over the place.

"What do they call you?"

"I'm not as cool as you, Strike. They call me, Shante. That's the name I was born with."

"I'm sure I could come up with a nickname for you by the end of the night."

"I bet you could."

"Why don't I help you take your mind off this fucked up day?"

"How might you do that, Strike?"

He leans over and whispers in my ear. "I have ways." He licks his lips.

"I have no doubt."

"Why don't we go get you some dinner?"

"I need to take care of something on campus, maybe some other time."

"I'm going to hold you to that, Beautiful."

"Okay."

He stands and reaches for my hand. I have no idea why. "It was nice to meet you," he says.

"You too." I extend my hand, and he places a delicate kiss on my knuckles.

He walks away, and I'm a little relieved, but I do take the time to appreciate him in all his sexiness.

II ~ Jeremiah

My mind is seriously fucked up. This can't be happening, but the wolf is clear, adamant, damn near impossible to control. He wants Shante. That woman is my fated mate. That's too damn bad. He's going to have to get over it. There's no way in hell I'm mating her. Somebody made a mistake. Still, the beast keeps pushing me to mate, and he's persistent. He's angered by my resistance and won't allow me to concentrate on anything else.

The moment she walked through the door, I was drawn to her. I won't deny she's beautiful, but she's also loud, obnoxious, and crass. She has no respect for me. She tried to undermine me in front of my class. I had to physically pick her up to get rid of her. Where the hell did she come from? And how the hell did she end up in front of me?

I can't think about that. I have to focus on my class. If they had seen me in the hallway, they'd probably question why I was hired as a professor. I've never behaved that way before. I'm always professional. She already has me out of character. I've worked too hard to get where I am. I don't need her kind of distraction.

I take a deep breath as I step into the classroom. "Pardon the interruption. We have rules for a reason." I lean against my desk. "I assure you all I'm not just being an ass."

There are a few chuckles.

"I was about to get to that before we were interrupted. When dealing with legal matters, time is of the utmost importance. The legal system is structured with rules, procedures, and deadlines. There's no way to avoid it. Your clients' livelihoods and freedom are on the line. You can't be late with court documents or for hearings. No one will care about your excuses. You will lose, and the client will suffer. Does everyone understand me?"

"Yes," the students reply.

"You may call me, Professor Johnson."

"Yes, Professor Johnson," they say.

"Professionalism is important in the legal field, and as my students, you will conduct yourselves as professionals in my classroom. Using slang will not be tolerated. Understood?"

"Yes, Professor Johnson."

"I know other professors offer grace periods and extensions, but I do not. You will be expected to meet all deadlines. If you cannot make it here to turn in an assignment, you are expected to email it, send it by messenger. I don't care. Do whatever you need to do to get it to me because you're responsible for getting the job done. Also, attendance will be ten percent of your grade. I'm always available if you need help. My office hours and contact information are located on the first page of your syllabus." I hand a stack of papers to someone on the front row, and they pass them down.

"How many of you are in the Paralegal Studies Associates Degree program?" A majority of the students lift their hands.

"Very good. You've chosen a wonderful career, and I wish you luck. If any of you are thinking about dropping this course, I want to make sure you understand something." I see the fear in their eyes as they wait for my next words. "There are only two legal teachers here, and I'm the only one who teaches Intro to Law. There's no way to avoid me, so you may as well stick around. I won't hold you all long tonight. I expect you to read the first two chapters and be able to define the legal terms. Answer the questions at the end of each chapter, and be prepared to turn them in on Wednesday. Class participation is a big part of your grade, and discussion will be a big part of this class. You may refer to your syllabus for all other important details, including how to turn in assignments. You will learn legal documents are important and must be formatted correctly and error free. I'm getting you prepared ahead of time. For now, you are dismissed. Have a good night."

I planned on lecturing tonight, but my mind is consumed with Shante Wilson, tempting me with that short blue skirt and that tight white shirt, swaying her hips as she walked into my classroom late. All I can think about is her big, sexy thighs and squeezing her juicy ass. I want to grab her. I want to bend her over my desk. I want to mark her, but there's one problem. I could never be with her. It looks like I'll have to find my own mate, because she is not the one for me. That doesn't stop my dick from swelling when I think about her big, beautiful lips, her caramel skin, or her long, thick brown hair. And her eyes, her big, bright eyes could bring me to my knees.

I nod as my students file out of the classroom with salutations. I recognize some familiar faces and quite a few new students. I'm pleased that the paralegal program keeps growing. Once everyone is gone, I sit at my desk and scratch my chin.

"MATE!" My wolf demands.

"Shit. What am I going to do?"

"That's exactly what I was thinking."

That voice. It's her. My heart jumps. I stare into her eyes. "Miss Wilson."

"Jeremiah," she says.

12

This is the problem. No respect. She drives me crazy, but my body betrays my mind. Every part of me is aware of her presence. The sound of my name on her lips is music to my ears, and her scent intoxicates me. "Call me, Professor Johnson, Miss Wilson."

"Call me, Shante," she says.

"I thought you left."

"You thought that after the way you behaved, I'd run away. Is that what you were hoping?"

"The way I behaved? You can't be serious."

"You picked me up and tossed me outside like trash, Jeremiah."

I'm ready to protest, but the look on her face destroys me. She's hurt, sad, defeated. I was expecting more banter. She seemed like she was ready for a fight. I had no idea she was sensitive or that I was such a jackass. At the time, I saw nothing wrong with my behavior, but now that I think about it, no matter how she got under my skin, I was wrong. I never behave that way, and I'm ashamed of myself. I rise from my desk and stand next to her.

Her head is bowed.

I think about comforting her, but I wrestle with myself, moving my hand back and forth before I rest it on her arm. Electricity flows through my body. This connection is too much for me. "Shante, I apologize." I can see she's holding back tears. My heart breaks. I don't make a habit of making women cry.

There's sudden determination in her eyes. She holds out her index finger and pokes my shoulder. "You had no right to treat me that way," she says.

My eyes widen. I take steps backward as she advances. "You refused to listen. You were being impossible."

"That doesn't make it okay. You think you're better than me. You think you can treat me like I'm beneath you. You and your fancy sweater can go to hell. Don't you ever put your hands on me again," she shouts.

I look around. I'm literally backed into a corner. I deserve her chastisement. Damn. I grab her hands and hold them down.

She's startled, and I can scent her arousal.

"I won't do it again, Shante. I hope you can forgive me."

"Hell no."

It's hard for me to resist the urge to be close to her. I rub her wrists. "Shante."

She turns her head away from me.

"Look at me, Shante."

"I acted impulsively, and I'm sorry. I'm ashamed of my behavior. You deserve nothing but my respect."

Her face tells me my words affect her. After a few moments, she speaks. "I'm not falling for this. You're only saying that because you don't want me to report you."

"You have every right to report me. If you choose to do so, I'll do nothing to stop you. I'll face whatever consequences come along with that, okay."

"Whatever," she says.

"I mean it."

"I don't want to report you. I don't know how things got so out of hand."

"You were disrespectful," I say.

"Your actions were over the top, but I should've listened to you as the professor."

"And I shouldn't have overreacted."

"No, you shouldn't have."

"Why don't we put it behind us and start over?" she asks.

"I'd like that," I say. I realize I'm still holding her hands.

I think she's aware too because she removes them from mine. I can't tell if the sweat in my palms is from me or her.

"I'll see you Wednesday," she says.

She walks away, leaving my wolf and me bereft. "Wait," I say.

14

She pauses, and I stand behind her, careful not to touch her but close enough to whisper in her ear. "You didn't accept my apology, Shante."

She trembles under my voice. She wants Big Daddy. "I'll accept it when I know you mean it." She faces me, and our eyes lock.

I look at her supple breasts and over the curves of her body. Her scent is like fresh berries, and I want to taste her juices. I can't deny she's sexy, but I'm determined to fight it.

"Why don't you sit?" I say.

"I don't know."

"Let me tell you what I went over during class. It's the least I can do, and it won't take long."

She sighs and looks at her watch.

I hold out my hand. If she walks away, she's not interested, and I'm free. I can forget about her, and we can move on.

She grabs my hand, and my heart skips a beat as I escort her to a chair. I give her another syllabus, sit on the edge of my desk. My focus is solely on her. I get lost in her eyes and for a moment, time stands still. When I compose myself, I give her the same speech I gave to the rest of the class.

"I get it," she says. "I promise I'm not usually late. I tried to get here on time. It's just been one of those days." She takes a frustrated breath and holds her head down. "I can't do this."

"Hold your head up, Miss Wilson."

She looks at me.

"You're stronger than this."

"I have a lot going on, but I'm trying."

I don't want to get emotionally involved, but I can't stand to see her hurt. I wrestle with myself over what to do. "Do you want to talk about it?" I ask.

"No, I'm sorry." She rises from her desk. "I should get going. Thank you."

—

She attempts to walk past me, and I take her arm and pull her close to me. I inhale her sweet scent as I embrace her. She needs me. The man in me wants to take her pain away as she cries into my chest. I rub her hair and hold her in my arms. I want to find out what's hurting her so I can fix it.

She wraps her arms around me.

My wolf appreciates her touch, and he's calmed down.

"It's going to be okay. I got you," I say. I kiss her forehead.

"You smell good," she says.

I smile to myself. I'm sure I smell good to her since she's my mate. What am I doing? I release my hold on her.

She pulls back and smiles through her tears.

Why is this happening to me? I can't stand to see her cry. I wipe her tears away and hold her cheek in my hand.

"I'm so embarrassed," she says. "I ruined your fancy sweater."

"Don't you worry about this sweater. I'm only worried about you, Miss Wilson. I want to make sure you're okay. Did somebody hurt you?"

"You mean, other than you?"

"Yes, other than me. Who do I need to set straight?"

"You?" she laughs.

"What's so funny?" I ask.

"You are uptight and proper. You're telling me you're going to throw hands."

"You're judging me?"

"Jeremiah, you're pretty easy to read. You don't get your hands dirty. You've got all these muscles, but have you ever been in a fight?"

"Wow," I say.

"I know, I know. Let me guess. You fight in the courtroom, right?" She laughs.

She's making fun of me. This woman drives me crazy, but she's laughing, so I don't bother getting pissed that it's at my expense. Her laugh is so ridiculously loud that I can't help but smile.

—

"You have a pretty smile," she says. "You should use it more often."

My arms are still wrapped around her. "If you laugh like that and look at me like this, I promise I'll smile more."

She beams. "I don't know what to say to that."

"You're at a loss for words? I find that hard to believe."

"Jeremiah, I should get going."

"I told you to call me Professor Johnson."

"I like to say your name. It's very official, sounds important."

"Can we negotiate?"

"Maybe, Jeremiah."

"I love to hear you say my name, but Professor Johnson, during class, okay."

"And what will you do for me?"

I graze her cheek with my finger. "I can think of a few things I want to do to you once class is dismissed."

Shante blushes. "I said for me."

"That too."

She turns her head and smiles. "I'm not sure what to make of that."

"You should go."

"Thanks for, well, you know," she says.

I nod. "My pleasure. Don't let me hold you up."

She looks back at me. "Goodnight, Jeremiah."

"Goodnight." I sit on the edge of my desk and listen to the rhythm of her heart as she walks away. My body needs a few minutes to calm down. This woman can't be my mate.

I sit behind my desk and place my head in my hands. Minutes go by, and a familiar scent enters the classroom. "What the hell are you doing here?" I say.

"Is that any way to greet your baby brother?"

Besides his height, my brother is the complete opposite of me physically. His skin is lighter, and he's

—
17

thinner. He looks like his mother, and I look like our father. "What do you want, William?"

"Why so formal? You know I don't go by William."

"I don't care what you go by. I only care that you leave my classroom. There's no way you're a student here."

"Our father requests your presence for dinner tonight at his home."

"Your father can't request shit from me. I'm never going to that house, and I can't believe you're asking me. You can get out."

"Look at you, Professor Johnson. Big shot attorney, looking down his nose at his own family. Your money, your house, and your cars don't make you better than us. We're your family."

"I have no family. I took care of myself with no help from any of you, so spare me the family bullshit."

"What beef do you have with me?" William asks. "It's been at least six months since I've seen you."

"You mean since your legal trouble."

"Yeah. Since my legal trouble. Sorry your baby brother is such a screw up. Is that why you haven't called me?"

"I didn't realize you were waiting for my call."

"You didn't even check on me."

"The phone works both ways."

"I know you didn't want to talk to me. I know you wish I weren't your brother."

"Look, I don't have beef with you, but you want to be him. I know what you and your father do, and I'm ashamed. You're lucky I don't turn you in."

"I don't have a choice."

"You've always had a choice. We all have choices in this. I choose not to kill. I choose not to poison our communities. I choose to build our people. You need to think about your choices in life."

"You're still my brother. You're supposed to have my back."

—
18

"I am your brother, but you are your father's son. Unless you tell me something's changed. Tell me you want to change your life, that you want to live up to your potential, and I'll help you. You can be so much more than you are, but I won't sit back and watch you destroy yourself. Nothing good can come from what you're doing."

"I'm not a lost soul that needs saving."

"You are. You just can't see it."

"Will you at least consider our father's offer. You know he doesn't like to hear no."

"I don't care what that man wants, and I'd better not find out you're dealing in my school. You stay away from here, and you stay away from me."

"I'll pass your message along."

I say nothing as my brother leaves my classroom.

III ~ Shante

What the hell was that? My mind races as I make my way to my car. I can't explain what's happening to me, to my body. Every part of me calls out to Jeremiah. I went back to the classroom to give him a piece of my mind, but somehow, I ended up in his arms. His embrace was warm, his touch, electrifying. I could've stayed in his arms all night. I felt comfortable there. I felt safe, and that's ironic considering his earlier behavior.

I thought he was cold and unforgiving, but he wiped away my tears. He told me everything would be alright, and I believed him. I think he kissed my forehead. My mind is so cloudy, I can't be sure. I shouldn't have gotten so carried away. There can't be anything between us.

I shake myself off as I walk to my car. I have two chapters to read by Wednesday. I have two classes tomorrow. Who knows how much work I'll have between my actual job and my other classes. One of them is algebra, and I hate math, which is why I avoided it the first time around. That's going to take up a lot of my time. I guess I should get as much reading done as I can tonight. I hope my other professors don't give too much work.

The journey to my car is over before I know it. I settle in my seat and lean my head against the headrest. I want to leave, but I need a moment to clear my head. It's been a hell of a day. I stick my key in the ignition and turn.

My car makes the most pathetic sound. Confused, I try several more times and get nothing.

"Come on, don't do this to me." I turn the key again. Maybe this time it'll do something different. "No, no, no," I shout as I hit the steering wheel with my palms.

I get out of the car. I want to scream. What the hell am I going to do? There's no one in the parking lot. I pull out my cellphone and call Brian. The phone rings, and my stomach sinks. "Please pick up. Please pick up," I beg. If there were ever a time I needed him to be reliable, it's now, but there's no answer. "Damnit," I shout. I try again. Nothing. I text him. *Please pick up your phone. I need help.*

Tears threaten to fall from my face. I have zero money, and there's no one else I can call. I try Brian several more times. He picks up four calls later.

"Hello," he says as if nothing is wrong.

"Brian, I've been calling you," I shout.

"I'm sorry. I sat my phone down. I just saw your call. What's going on?"

"Are you serious? I'm out here stranded, and you can't even pick up the phone. What the hell are you doing?"

"Don't start with all that. I'm on the phone now. What's up?"

"I'm stranded. Didn't you hear me?"

"Where are you?" He doesn't even sound concerned.

"Where do you think I am? I'm at school. My car won't start, and you won't answer the damn phone?"

"Stop yelling. What's wrong with the car?"

"If I knew that, I wouldn't have had to call you. Can you come up here and check it out?"

"I can't right now."

"Why not? What are you doing?"

21

"Look, can you get a ride home? I'll go look at it in the morning."

"Who am I going to get a ride from? I can't call a cab. I don't have any money. Can't you just come?"

"Let me see what I can do. I'll call you back."

"You can't be serious."

"Give me a few minutes."

"Do not hang up this phone, Brian."

"I'll call you back."

My eyes burn as he hangs up. That's the one thing I can count on, disappointment.

As always, I have to depend on myself. I open the car door and release the hood. I pry it open and look underneath. "Looks good to me." I let out a dry chuckle. I have no idea what I'm looking for. I must be losing it. I move to the side of the car and kick it.

"Damnit," I yell. "What's wrong with you? You stupid piece of junk. Ouch!" I hop around on one leg. I'm so done. I hop back to the car and hit the top. "You made me hurt my foot. Shit." It's getting dark outside. I hear the roar of a motorcycle driving by. I lay my head in my arm on top of the car. I no longer give a fuck. I want this day to be over.

"Excuse me." I hear a voice behind me, and my body freezes. His voice is already embedded in my brain, so deep and smooth. I know it's him.

"Jeremiah," I say. I take a deep breath and turn around. Where did he come from? "What's up?"

"I was going to ask you that. Car trouble?" he asks.

"It's nothing." I lie.

"Let me take a look."

He feels so familiar, it's hard for me to remember I don't know him at all. He's under no obligation to help me. "I'm sure there's nothing you can do. I already called my boyfriend. It's fine."

"Your boyfriend?"

If I didn't know better, I'd say he didn't like hearing that. "Yeah, he's going to see if he can come get me."

22

"What do you mean he's going to see?" His nostrils flare.

"Ummm, he's coming."

"You're lying to me."

"No, he was doing something, but he's coming."

His angry eyes draw me in. "Tell me the truth."

I'm so embarrassed, but I feel compelled to tell him the truth. His stare is powerful, and he seems to be able to read me. "He said he's going to call me back."

"How long ago was that?" Jeremiah asks.

"About twenty minutes ago."

"And has he called back?"

I remain silent.

"I asked you a question."

"Look, why are you questioning me? What are you even doing here?"

"Answer me."

"He hasn't."

"What's this guy's name?"

"Why?" I ask.

"Call him."

"What are you talking about?"

"Call him now. I want to talk to him."

"No. Are you crazy? I'm not doing that."

"He should've dropped whatever he was doing and been here. What kind of man leaves a woman stranded in the middle of the night? What if something happened to you?"

"I'm fine, as you can see. It's not completely dark yet. I don't need to be rescued."

"You're not fine, Shante."

"I am. Thank you for checking. You can go." Embarrassed doesn't begin to describe what I'm feeling at this moment.

"I'm not leaving you here alone. Are you out of your damn mind?"

Did he just snap at me? "I told you, he's coming," I say.

—

23

"I don't know if you're lying to yourself or me. This is not the guy for you."

"You don't have the right to say that."

He ignores me. "What's wrong with the car?"

"It wouldn't start."

"Turn the ignition for me."

I get inside and do as he says. It makes the same pathetic noise.

"Do you have gas?" he asks.

"Yes, I have gas." I roll my eyes and discreetly check the gauge. It's half full. I let out the breath I was holding.

He takes off his sweater. I just watch. He unbuttons his white shirt, and I gasp. He's wearing a fitted white tee, and I can't tear my eyes away from his bulging biceps or his pecs. There's a tattoo peeking underneath his sleeve. "Well, damn," I say. Maybe I was wrong about him.

"What was that?" he asks.

"Nothing."

He smirks. "Hold this for me." He hands me his shirts.

I can smell his scent. It's hard not to hold his shirts to my nose and sniff. I don't know what's come over me. I have a boyfriend. A little flirtation is harmless, but I can't sniff another man's shirt.

He walks closer to the car and looks under the hood. I'm not sure what I should do, so I sit and wait.

"Turn the ignition one more time."

I do, and it's the same pathetic noise.

"Pop the trunk for me."

I pop the trunk. I'm nervous because I can't remember what's in there.

Jeremiah ruffles through my belongings and comes back with jumper cables. He stops in front of me. "I'm pretty sure your battery is dead."

"Oh," I say as I lay my head against the headrest.

The next thing I know, he pulls to the front of my car on a motorcycle. My eyes bug out of my head. I sit his shirts in my passenger seat and jump out of the car.

"You drive a motorcycle?" I ask as he steps off the bike.

"Sometimes."

"I just thought—"

"You thought you had me figured out. You thought I was a lame, entitled asshole who's never worked hard a day in his life."

"No," I lie.

"Sure."

He takes the jumper cables and attaches them to our batteries.

"Get your ass back in the car," he says. "Turn the key when I give you the thumbs up."

I jump to do as he says. I'm not going to deny it, that was sexy.

He revs the engine of the bike. It's loud as hell. I want to cover my ears, but I hold out. He gives me the thumbs up, and I say a silent prayer as I turn the key. It worked. I can finally breathe.

Jeremiah is taking the cables back to my trunk when I get out of the car. "Thank you so much."

"It's not a problem. You should be able to make it home, but you're going to need to get the battery replaced."

I nod in agreement, but I'm upset. I feel like I'm back at square one.

"What's wrong?" he asks.

"It's not your problem."

"What is it?"

"You've been so helpful. I appreciate you. I really do."

"I'm glad I could help, now tell me what's wrong."

"Look, I can't do this."

"You can't do what, Shante?"

"Go back to school."

"Why did you sign up in the first place?"

I lean against the car. "I wanted to be like Erin Brockovich."

He laughs.

_____

25

"You're laughing at me?"

"No, I think it's sweet."

I throw my hands up. "You think it's stupid."

"No, Ms. Wilson. I think you could be like Erin Brockovich. What area of law are you interested in?"

"I don't know. I just want to help people."

"Don't lose sight of that. There are many areas of practice, but sometimes when you're starting, you have to take the job you can get until you gain experience. There's a lot of paperwork and long hours. It's not always glamorous. You understand?"

"Yeah, I understand. It doesn't matter anymore. I'm going to have to withdraw from school."

"Why?" He steps closer to me.

"Jeremiah," I sigh.

"Shante," his deep voice beckons me.

"It's none of your business."

"Well, you're quitting, so you won't see me again. What do you have to lose?"

"My dignity."

"Talk to me."

"I used every dime I had to register for class and buy books, and now everything's falling apart. I couldn't get financial aid. My bank account is overdrawn. I thought I could hang on, but now, I need a battery. I feel like I'm drowning. I don't know what I'm going to do. Maybe this wasn't the right time." I shake my head. "Anyway, thank you for helping me. I guess this is goodbye."

"If you quit now, you'll never do it."

"No, I will. It'll just be later."

He looks angry. "You're a spoiled brat."

"Excuse me," I shout.

"Nothing worth having comes easily. Things get a little tough, and your instinct is to give up?"

"No."

"That's exactly what you're doing. Stop feeling sorry for yourself."

"You don't even know me."

—
26

"Do you have a roof over your head?" he asks.

"Yes."

"You're already here. Find a way. My mate is not a quitter. You want to be Erin Brockovich, well, she didn't give up, and you're not either. So, if you need to go home and feel sorry for yourself, do it, but I'd better see your ass in class on Wednesday, at six o'clock sharp. Do I make myself clear?"

I flinch. "Yeah."

"Good. Let's get out of here."

"Okay." I'm reluctant to say anything else.

"Where do you live?" he asks.

"Why?"

"I'm going to make sure you get home."

"No, you've done enough. I'll be okay."

"I'm not asking. If your boyfriend's not going to make sure you're safe, I am."

"Jeremiah, I know you're trying to help, but it's okay."

"Either call your boyfriend and make sure he comes, or I'm following you."

"Fine, I'll call him."

"Do it now," he says.

I grab my phone and call Brian. I'm relieved when he actually answers. I don't want to be further embarrassed in front of Jeremiah. "Brian," I say.

"Hey, baby."

"I got the car running."

"Good, I was about to call you."

"Really? What were you going to say?"

"It doesn't matter now. You got the car running. Call me and let me know when you've made it home."

"You don't even want to know what was wrong?"

"What was it?"

"I need a battery."

"That's not bad. You can get a battery."

"Thanks. That's helpful, Brian."

"Let me know when you make it."

"What if something happens on the way?"

—

27

"Then you call me."

"Why would I even bother?" I hang up.

"Do you know what your problem is?" I almost forgot Jeremiah was there.

"What?" I shout.

"Brian is your problem. He's holding you back."

I begin to protest, but he cuts me off.

"Let's get going."

"You don't have to follow me. I have a stop to make before I go home."

"Where's that?"

"Why are you all in my business?"

"Where?"

"I have to go visit my grandmother."

"Now?"

"I don't expect you to go. I promised I'd go see her when I got out of class.'"

"You're wasting time." He closes the hood.

I throw my hands up and get behind the wheel. I can't help but look at his body as he settles on his motorcycle.

I drive fifteen minutes to my grandmother's house, and Jeremiah is right behind me, watching over me, protecting me. I've never had anyone do that before. I get out of the car, and he gets off his bike.

IV ~ Jeremiah

Shante thinks I'm about to leave, but she's wrong. The least I can do is make sure she makes it home, and that's what I'm going to do. Her grandmother has a charming one-story, brick house that's nicely landscaped. There are beautiful flowers planted in the front yard that remind me of Shante, vibrant and full of life.

"Thank you, Jeremiah," she says.

"You're welcome."

"I'm going to go see my grandma."

"I'll wait here."

She sighs. "Jeremiah."

"I said, I'll wait here." I can tell she doesn't want to argue with me.

"Why don't you come inside and wait?"

"If you insist." I follow her inside.

Most of the lights are off, but the blue glare of the television blinks, giving bursts of illumination throughout the room. Doesn't matter, though. I don't have a problem seeing in the dark.

Her grandmother's home is comfortable and full of memories. Family photos grace the walls of the entrance. Photos of Shante and her family make this home feel warm. I take in as much as I can. She looks the same as she did in her high school graduation photos.

Her grandmother sits facing the television.

"Nana, why aren't you in bed?" Shante asks as she turns on the lights and gives her grandmother a hug.

I don't want to interrupt their moment so I stand against the wall.

"I'm not tired. It's still early her grandmother says.

"Not for you, it's not. You need to rest."

"Child, I'll rest when I'm dead."

"That's not funny, Nana."

"Loosen up, girl. I am resting."

"How are you feeling today?"

"I'm feeling just fine."

"Did you walk around?"

"That ain't none of your business."

"Nana."

"That's right. I'm your Nana. I tell you what to do. You don't tell me what to do."

I laugh to myself. She's sitting in a chair with a blanket covering her lap. She's beautiful, just like Shante. But her hair's grey, and her body's frail. She's definitely feisty, but she's sick. I can scent it. My heart breaks for Shante.

"Who did you bring into my house?" her grandmother asks.

"This is my friend, Jeremiah, Nana. I was having car trouble, and he helped me out."

I step forward. "It's a pleasure to meet you, ma'am. I'm Jeremiah Johnson. What can I call you?"

She looks delighted. "Call me, Mable, handsome," she says.

I extend my hand and take hers in mine as I bend my knees to offer her a kiss. "You have a beautiful home, Miss Mable," I say. "I love your flowers. They brighten up your lawn."

She beams. "Thank you, Jeremiah. I picked those out myself. I used to garden when I was able to move these old

—
30

bones. I got the tulips because Shante loves tulips. Now, my baby, Shante, takes care of my garden for me."

"Shante is certainly special." I look at her, and she blushes.

"You love her," she says.

"Nana," Shante jumps in, her eyes wide. "It's not like that, Nana."

"Hush, child. I know what I see. I'm glad you found him. He's a good man."

"Nana, we don't even know one another."

"Child, that don't matter. Love grows like those flowers in my garden out there. It starts as a seed, then it blooms, then it blossoms into something beautiful. Isn't that right, Jeremiah?"

"Yes, ma'am. It is," I say.

"You're embarrassing me," Shante says.

"No sense in being embarrassed."

"Could you please stop."

"Shante, baby, go to the back and read that article I left in your room for you."

"I think I should stay out here, Nana."

"Lil' Girl, I said, go. I want to talk to your young man."

"But Nana, he's not—"

"Don't make me have to tell you again."

"Yes, ma'am," Shante says as she walks away with reluctance. She looks at me apologetically and I nod assuring her I'll be okay.

"Is that how you get her to mind?" I ask.

"She's hard headed."

"I noticed."

"You can handle her," she says.

"You know we're not together, don't you?"

"I know, but she doesn't know I know." She laughs. The same contagious laugh Shante has, but lighter.

I smile.

"You're a shifter, aren't you?" she asks.

Her question catches me off guard. "Ma'am?"

"Don't play coy with me. What are you? Werewolf?"

"Yes, ma'am."

"Are you an alpha?"

"Yes, ma'am."

"What's your pack?"

"Blue Ridge."

"And is your pack behaved."

"Yes, ma'am."

"I don't want my granddaughter hurt."

"I wouldn't let anything happen to her."

"Good. Take your time with her, and be patient."

"Nana, I don't know about that."

"That boyfriend that she has is no good for her. She needs you, and she'll come to see that."

"It's not that simple."

"Isn't she your mate?"

"Nana."

"She'll come around. She fights hard because she loves harder."

"How do you know these things?"

"I'm an old woman who's lived quite a life. I know a shifter when I see one."

"I see where Shante gets that fire."

"That's right, and don't you forget it. She comes from a line of strong women. Her life hasn't been easy, but she's come a long way."

"What do you mean?"

"Her father was not a good man. He left her and her mother with nothing to fend for themselves. Then, he was killed when she was a toddler. Shante never got to know him. Her mother brought her to stay with me when she was six, and she hasn't been a big part of her life since. That daughter of mine. Always chasing after some loser or some dream or some high. She chases anything but her own damn daughter. After Shante's grandfather died, it's just been her and me."

"I had no idea."

She grabs my hand and squeezes.

—

32

I look into her eyes, and I know we understand one another. "Nana, how much time do you have left?" I ask.

"Not much. She's going to need you. She acts like everything is fine. I think she's in denial. She doesn't want me to worry about her. She's stubborn, and she won't admit it when she needs help, because she doesn't want to depend on anyone."

"I've already experienced that."

She chuckles. "She thinks she'll be okay, but I know it's going to be rough. Just be there for her, and promise me something."

"Anything."

"Promise me you'll take care of my baby."

"I promise, Nana."

"Thank you."

"Who are you?" I ask.

"Ha, ha, that's a story for another time, Jeremiah. I'll tell you next time I see you."

"Promise," I say.

"Promise."

"I'm glad to have met you," I say, and I mean it. I love this lady.

"Most men usually are, dear."

I smile. "I think Shante is getting anxious in there," I say.

"Why don't you go on back there and get her? Take your time. I'm an old woman. I can't hear too good."

I make my way to the back. I can scent Shante, so I know which room she's in. I open the door and find her sitting on the bed. "Shante," I say.

She jumps. Her hand covers her chest.

"I didn't mean to startle you." I step inside.

"What are you doing in here?"

"I wanted to let you know it was safe to come back," I say. I look at her room. Her walls are a tribute to the best hip hop and R&B music from the nineties. Shante is smiling and laughing in all her photos with her friends and family. I imagine she had lots of friends growing up.

"I like your room," I say.

"Thank you. Nana left it like this for me. It brings back so many memories. We had no idea that life was so easy back then." She points to a photo. Four girls are doing various elaborate poses. She's in the middle with one knee on the ground and her hands out. "Those were my girls. We thought we were going to be the next TLC, with an extra member." She laughs.

I smile as I study the photo. I touch the spot where she stands. "Can you sing?"

"No," she laughs. "None of us could, but that wasn't going to stop us. We didn't have to be great singers as long as we weren't terrible."

"Of course. The music industry is full of not terrible singers."

"We would pretend we were making music videos, singing into our hairbrushes." She sings into her fist, like it's a microphone, and bobs her head from left to right. "We were like, baby, baby, baby," she began the classic TLC song.

I can't contain my laughter. "You really can't sing," I say.

"No, but I can rap," she laughs.

There's something about the way she looks at me. "It's nice to see you laugh," she says.

"It's nice to laugh," I say.

"What did your bedroom look like?" she asks.

"I had computers and gadgets, lots of clothes, but the walls were white and bare. My father was very strict. If you think I'm uptight, you have no idea."

"So, you couldn't decorate?"

"No. Decorating my room was a frivolous waste of time. A man has more important things to worry about. No time for bullshit."

"Is he the reason you became successful?"

"You think I'm successful?"

"I assume you are. You look successful. You act successful. You have a law degree. You're a professor."

"I became successful despite my father. He was an awful man, not an ounce of compassion, ruthless, and he wanted me to be like him."

"But you're not. You're a good guy."

"I'm glad you think so."

"That must've sucked."

"Nothing I did was ever good enough, but it's okay. I reached a breaking point when I was seventeen. I left his home. I put myself through college, and I haven't seen him since."

"I'm sorry," she says.

"It's okay," I say. I can't believe I told her those things. I haven't spoken about my father in all these years.

"It's not okay. I didn't have my parents, but at least I had my Nana. She was firm when she needed to be and loving when she needed to be."

"Your Nana is amazing. You're lucky to have her. Speaking of, we should get back."

"You're right," she says.

I inhale her sweet scent as she walks past me, and her body brushes against mine. I take a deep breath before following her.

"Is everything okay in here?" Shante asks.

"I'm just watching my show," Nana says. "Listen, Jeremiah, make sure you come see me again."

"I would love that. I'll be back soon."

"Nana, he can't," Shante says.

Nana changes the subject. "How was your first day at school?"

"It wasn't what I expected," Shante says.

"What happened?" Nana asks Shante.

"I got kicked out of class."

"Were you running your mouth again?" Nana asks.

"Why don't you ask him?" Shante points to me. "Your precious friend is the one who kicked me out."

"You're the professor?"

"Yes, ma'am."

"You two be careful. I don't want you getting into trouble."

"We will," I say.

"Why did you put my baby out of class?" Nana asks.

Shante looks at me like she's won a victory.

"She was late," I say.

"Girl, why was you late? I know I taught you better than that."

"I was barely late. It wasn't fair."

"Life is not fair, little girl. It's your responsibility to be to class on time. It's his classroom, his rules. I'm sure he has a reason for the way he does things. You have to respect that. You hear me?"

"Yes, ma'am," Shante says. "It's been an awful day. I had work and traffic, and I was almost there, but someone ran into me."

Nana shakes her head. "We don't make excuses. Just do better." She looks at me. "How long you been teaching at that school?"

"Three years."

"Do you teach full-time?"

"No, ma'am. I'm a lawyer."

"Shut the front door. What kind of law do you practice?"

"Corporate. I'm head of the legal department at Alpha Security Corporation."

"Shante, don't you let this man get away, now. He's a good man. My baby got her a lawyer." Nana is pleased. "A lawyer and a pa—. What's that you're going to school for?"

"Paralegal, Nana."

"A lawyer and a paralegal." She clasps her hands together.

"Nana, it's time for you to go to bed. Come on, let's go," Shante says.

"I was talking to Jeremiah."

"You can talk to him later. He'll be back, remember."

"Okay. I guess, but don't you forget. Okay, Jeremiah."

36

"I won't forget, Nana."

"Let's go." Shante helps her to her bedroom.

I adore Nana, and even though I'd love to talk to her some more, I want to give them some time alone, so I wait for Shante outside.

The moon shines bright, and I resist the urge to howl as Shante is on my mind. Hours ago, my decision was clear. I was not going to accept Shante as my mate. Now things are foggy. She's gotten under my skin.

The door closing interrupts my thoughts. There's a shy smile on Shante's face as the wind breezes through her hair. She looks so gentle, so kind, so beautiful, illuminated by the moonlight. "Come to me, my mate," I whisper. The look in her eyes. I can sense her nervous energy. We're drawn to one another. My wolf presses against my skin. I feel my eyes change. I reach for her, and she grabs my hand. My body tingles at the touch of her delicate skin.

"Jeremiah, I'm sorry," she begins.

"Shhh." I pull her close to me and inhale the scent of sweet berries, and before she can say anything, I kiss her. She doesn't resist. Her soft lips press against mine, and her head leans to the side. I take my time and study her lips. She's gentle in this moment. It's the sweetest kiss I've ever experienced. An electric current flows from her lips through my body as I capture her mouth and her tongue. Time stands still, and it feels like hours have passed when we pull apart.

"I'm not sorry," I say. My finger brushes her cheek.

"That was—"

"I know."

"Can I ask you something?" she asks.

"You just did."

"Very funny," she says. "What does it feel like to ride on a motorcycle?"

"It feels like you're flying. Your mind clears, and it's just you and the wind."

"That sounds perfect."

"Do you want to ride?" I ask.

"Really?"

"Yes." I lead her to my bike and give her a helmet.

"I don't know," she says.

"I know you're not scared," I say.

"I'm not." She puts the helmet on, but I can feel her nervous energy.

I mount the bike and pat the spot behind me. "Get on. Don't be nervous. I won't let anything happen to you."

"I trust you," she says, warming my heart.

"Hold on tight," I say.

"Where?"

"My shoulders or my waist."

She wraps her arms around my waist.

"Relax."

She loosens her grip. I start the bike, and her fingers dig into my skin when I peel off. I take her out of the neighborhood so that my bike doesn't disturb her grandmother's neighbors. When we're on the road, her body relaxes. She lays her head against my back, and I feel like a champion.

"This is nice," she says.

"Do you want to go faster?" I yell.

"Hell yeah."

I speed up. She stiffens at first, but then, she lets go of my waist and moves her hands to my shoulders. She holds one hand out to catch the wind.

"Jeremiah," she shouts. "I love this."

"I know," I shout.

She lays her head on my back and squeezes me tight. I like this feeling, so I drive her around a while longer.

"We're going to head back," I say.

I take her closer to the neighborhood and slow down.

"I wish we could do this again," she says.

"Who says we can't?"

"Pull over here."

I pull into the park down the street from her grandmother's house. "Are you okay?" I ask as I get off the bike.

—

38

She takes off her helmet. "I'm fine. I just want to pause for a minute. I don't want to hold you up though."

"I don't mind."

She pushes her body forward and leans in, grabbing the handlebars.

I can't help but stare at her curves molded perfectly against my bike. Her skirt is lifted, exposing her entire thigh and then some. Damn, she's sexy.

"Can you take a picture of me?"

Her question catches me off guard. "Yes, sure." I take out my cellphone. She tosses her hair and smiles at me, and I snap the picture. I look at the image. "You're a natural," I say.

She lights up as I walk over and show it to her. "Take one with me," she says.

I sigh.

"Please," she says.

I hand her my phone. She turns on the selfie camera. I look at us on the screen and smile. That's when she snaps the photo.

"It looks good. You're smiling," she says.

"It does look good," I say.

"It's been a hell of a day, and thanks to you, I feel so much better. I just want to be here, in this moment, a little longer."

"I feel the same way."

"Do you want to get on the swings?" she asks.

"No."

"I assume you're too sophisticated to partake in such childish activities."

"Correct."

"Are you sure? It feels like flying."

"I'm sure."

"Come on. Your dad would hate it."

She grabs my hand and leads me to the swings. "When I was trying to forget about the noise in my head, about why the other kids had parents and I didn't, about why I felt so alone, I would come here."

"I'm sorry about that."

She shrugs. "It is what it is."

I sit on the swing and pull her into my lap. She wraps her arms around me from the side and lays her head on my shoulder. I use the power of my legs to push us back, and the swing takes off. She looks at me with amazement as we move back and forth. I let the swing slow naturally as I'm compelled to kiss her lips. We come to a stop as I look into her eyes.

"I don't swing," I say.

"It'll be our little secret," she says.

She snuggles against my chest. I rub her hair and kiss her forehead.

We sit for a while. I'm at peace. Being here, with her in my arms, I understand why my wolf doesn't want to let her go. I howl at the moon. She's startled. She looks at me like I've lost my mind and howls too. She doesn't make fun of me or question my sanity. She just smiles. That's when I know.

"We should head back," I say.

"Okay."

I take her back to Nana's house. I walk her to her car and open the door. "Let's get you home."

She climbs in and looks up. Her eyes are wide with passion and confusion.

I make sure she's seated safely before I close the door. "Start the car," I say. "I want to make sure it's still running."

She does.

"I'm right behind you," I say.

I get on my bike and follow her as she heads down the street.

She lives in an apartment complex, not far from Nana's house. I hate that she lives here, and I hate there's nothing I can do about it. This neighborhood isn't safe. There are questionable characters everywhere I look. Groups of so-called men hanging around outside, watching everything that's going on. I'm aware of them all, and I could scent what they wanted when they saw Shante pull up. I want nothing more than to take her home with me where she belongs.

I open her car door. She grabs her books and purse and stands next to me. "I'm walking you to the door," I say as I take her books and grab her by the waist. I want to make sure anyone who sees us knows she's mine. I wish someone would challenge me, so they'll know I'm not to be fucked with, and neither is Shante. I grab her keys, as well. She might want to protest, but I don't give her a chance.

"I'm okay with that," she says.

"Which way?" I ask.

She lives on the first floor of this dimly lit complex. The landscaping isn't kept up. The building has seen better days, and while it's not the worst place in the world, it's not good enough for my Shante.

When we reach the door, she turns to me and smiles. "There are no words," she says.

"I can't believe you don't have words."

"Thank you for everything. My Nana loves you. I didn't have the heart to tell her it wasn't real."

"It is real."

"What do you mean?"

"Kiss me again, and tell me it's not real."

She can't resist the urge, and neither can I. Our lips meet once again. This time more urgently. I push her against the door and dominate her mouth. I'm sure she can feel my desire against her leg. The scent of her need is powerful, and my wolf wants to mate, right here, right now. She holds on to my body like she can't get enough of me. My free hand slips underneath her skirt. I feel her cotton panties and rip them from her body. "Mine." I growl.

She moans in response.

"You are mine, Shante. Your body is mine. Your heart is mine. Do you understand?"

She moans again.

"I asked you a question."

"Ask me again."

I sit her books on the ground and turn her around. Her back is to me. Her arms pent up over her head. My free hand explores her curves before reaching underneath her skirt once more. "Tell me you're mine."

"Jeremiah," she whispers.

"I won't settle for anything less." I grab her ass and squeeze, then reach between her legs and flick my finger. I hear her juices and feel her body yearning. "See how wet you are for me? That's mine," I say. "Tell me."

"I'm yours."

The wolf pushes against my skin, and I'm forced to remove my hand. My claws extend. I lightly scratch her leg. Make no mistake, I plan to mark her, but not tonight. My canines extend, but I must resist the urge to bite. Once I regain control I kiss her neck before I pull away.

She faces me. The look in her eyes is hungry.

"I should go."

"Jeremiah, I'm lightheaded."

I pick her books up off the ground.

"Jeremiah. I have a boyfriend. I shouldn't have done that."

"What's a boyfriend?"

"Brian. He and I are together," she says.

"That won't last much longer," I reply.

"I'm sorry. This was wrong."

"What do you want a boyfriend for? I'm not trying to be your boyfriend."

She hangs her head. "Oh, right."

I know what she's thinking. She thought I was different, but it's clear I'm like every other man. I hold her head up by her chin, and I make sure my eyes look straight into hers, so there's no confusion. "I want my mate, my wife, the mother of my children. So, no. I don't want to be your boyfriend. You let me know when you're ready for a man." I unlock her door and hand her the keys. I leave her with a kiss on the cheek, make sure she gets inside, and wish her goodnight.

She's speechless as I close the door and walk away.

When I get back to my bike, I stand next to it with my arms folded and look. I watch everyone and everything around me. My head held high, my feet shoulder width apart. I know all eyes are on me. I want to see if anyone here has the courage to approach me. As I suspected, no one bothers. There are whispers from those who wonder who I am, where I came from, or who I work for, but they don't know me, and they don't want to.

V ~ Shante

Who am I kidding? Sleep was out of the question for me the moment Jeremiah walked away. My body begged him to stay, but I couldn't bring myself to ask. He kissed me. He touched me, and I've never felt so alive. I sit up in my bed and rub my fingers over my mouth. I can still feel his lips pressed against mine, remnants from the best kiss of my life. My skin tingles when I think about his touch.

There's just one problem. I'm a low down, dirty cheater. What am I going to do about my boyfriend? Thoughts of Brian fade as Jeremiah consumes my mind. He's everything I've never had, everything I never thought I would have, and everything I could ever want. Maybe yesterday was a dream. I didn't think men like him existed. He showed up, and he came through for me. He met my grandmother, and she loved him.

My thoughts are interrupted by a knock on the door. *Who could that be?* I look at my phone. It's early. I jump out of bed and put on my robe. My heart skips a beat when I look through the peephole. It's Jeremiah. I run to the microwave and squint to see my reflection in the glass. I smooth my hair as best I can. My heart feels like it's about to burst through my chest.

I calm myself as I open the door. "Jeremiah, what are you doing here?"

"I brought you something," he says. He's wearing a dark blue, tailored suit that showcases his muscular body. I want to grab that skinny tie and pull him close to me. His scent intoxicates me, and that golden color flashes in his eyes.

"What did you bring me?" I ask.

"Hold out your hand."

I reluctantly hold it out my hand. He kisses it and places my car key in my palm. "How did you get this?"

"I took it off your key chain last night. It turns out your battery was still under warranty. It's been replaced, and you're good to go. It won't cost you anything."

"You stole my car. I don't know whether to slap you or hug you."

He looks over my body like he wants to devour me. "You can thank me by telling me what's underneath this robe." He steps inside my apartment and looks around. "I'll settle for a hug."

I was hoping he'd say that. I stand on my tiptoes and wrap my arms around his neck as the door closes. I sniff him as he squeezes my body and pulls me closer. "Thank you, Jeremiah."

"You're welcome, baby." I feel his lips on my neck. My body tightens, and a spark flows through me as he showers me with gentle kisses. "You're not wearing anything under here," he whispers as he runs his fingers over the fabric of my robe.

"I wasn't expecting company."

"You sleep naked?" he asks.

"Sometimes."

"Did you touch yourself while you were thinking of me last night?"

The scruff under his chin tickles my neck. "Who says I was thinking of you?"

"I know you were."

"Aren't you cocky?"

45

"I'm not wrong."

"I did think of you."

"Mm-hmm."

"And I did touch myself. I wanted to feel your hands all over my body. I wanted to feel your lips and your tongue all over my body." I reach for the front of his pants and grab his hardened length. I wanted this. Bad."

"Badly," he says.

"Correcting my English is so sexy," I joke.

He unties my robe, and the air hits my skin. So do his hands. They electrify my body as my robe falls to the floor. "How badly?"

"My body was calling you. I wish I had invited you inside. Did you want me as badly as I wanted you, Jeremiah?"

"I did. I do."

"What did you think of?"

"Fucking you until you begged for mercy. Owning you, claiming you, marking you, making you mine."

"I don't even know what that means, but I love it. No one's ever talked to me that way."

"You've never met a man like me."

"I know," I say. He picks me up, and I wrap my legs around his waist. "I've never felt anything like this."

His fingers sink into my ass, and he takes my breast into his mouth. He sucks my nipple, one and then the other. I need him. All he has to do is unzip his pants and slide inside me. I'm ready.

"Jeremiah, I need you."

"You have me," he says. He loosens his grip, and I slide down his body, ready for what comes next.

"Do you mean that?" I ask as I look into his eyes.

"I mean it, Beautiful. You're coming home with Big Daddy where you belong. You'll be my mate, my wife. You're going to finish school and have my babies. Do you want that?"

I blush as I nod. I must have lost my mind. I know better than to believe empty promises from a man, but I can't help but get excited. I believe Jeremiah "When?" I ask.

"Right away, Beautiful. I need you to do one thing first," he says.

"What?" I ask.

"Break up with Brian."

"Right." I'm stunned. I forgot about my boyfriend again. This suddenly feels like real life. Of course, I need to break up with Brian. I should've broken up with him a long time ago, but that's easier said than done.

"I'm not sharing you with another man. No one else can claim what's mine."

"I'm yours?" I ask.

He touches my cheek, and I shiver. "Yes, you're mine, and only mine for the rest of your life."

"I would love to believe you, but I don't know you, Jeremiah."

"That will change with time."

"How do I know that? How do I know this isn't just some fling?"

"No," he replies.

"No, what?" I ask.

"You're not going to question me. You're going to have faith in me, believe in me, love me."

"Love you." My heart beats rapidly.

"Yes, my mate."

"What do you mean? My mate?"

"I mean, you're mine for the rest of your life. I'm not going to tell you again. Don't you want to be mine?"

My eyes follow his lips. "Yes." I don't know what's come over me. "I want to be yours. Am I crazy?"

"No."

"Are you crazy?" I ask him.

"I know what I want. What do you want?"

"I want to be with you. I want to break up with him. I've thought about it before, but every time I try, I freeze."

"Get over it, and do it," he says.

"I love it when you take charge." I bite my lip and bat my eyelashes.

He growls.

I stand on my tiptoes, and my lips reach for a kiss.

"No," his head dodges my lips. "Not until it's over."

He shot me down. Hell no. I wrap my hands around his neck and press my naked body against him. "But you look so sexy, and you smell so good, and I want to feel your strong hands on my naked body."

"I want to give you this strong dick."

"You can't tease me like that."

"Call him and get it over with, now. Then I can give you what you want," he says.

"That's not fair," I say. My stomach churns. I want Jeremiah badly, but I'm scared to break up with Brian. I think I'm afraid of his reaction. I don't want him to try to convince me to stay with him. Even though I don't know Jeremiah, what I feel is undeniable.

"All is fair in love and war," he says.

"Do you think this is love?" I ask.

"I don't have doubts about what this is."

"You sound so sure."

"You can't avoid doing what you need to do, and I need to get to work."

"I'll do it today. I promise. Just give me till after work."

"Fine. I'll call you after work."

"Can I have a kiss for good luck?"

"No."

"Please."

"No."

I give him my best puppy dog eyes.

He gives me a peck on the lips.

I pull him closer and hold on tight. He holds me close, and I jump into his arms again. I want him, and my desire for him can't be quenched. I kiss him. I capture his tongue with my teeth and suck. I rub my hands over any part of

---

his body I can reach. My head rolls back as he kisses my neck and chest. I loosen his tie.

"What the fuck are you doing?" A voice booms through my apartment. A six-foot-tall, brown-skinned man comes charging into the room like a raging bull. His brown eyes seethe with anger.

"Brian, what are you doing here?" I yell.

"This is Brian," Jeremiah says as he puts me down.

I cover my body with my hands. I'm mortified. Jeremiah gives me his jacket, and I put it over my shoulders.

"Brian, this isn't what it looks like."

"It looks like I walked in on you fucking somebody else. Who is this?" he yells.

Jeremiah steps forward. "Shante is mine."

"Fuck you mean, she's yours?" Brian gets in Jeremiah's face.

"You don't deserve Shante. You've mistreated and neglected her. She needs a man to take care of her. You can go now before I remove you."

"I'm not going anywhere." Brian pushes Jeremiah, but Jeremiah doesn't budge.

I gasp as Jeremiah pulls me behind him and grabs Brian by the throat.

Brian struggles to break free of his grasp.

"Jeremiah," I yell.

"Don't you ever put your hands on me again. I will kill you." Jeremiah pushes, and Brian stumbles backward, falling to the floor. It takes him a moment to find his balance and jump to his feet.

"Shante, you'd better tell me what the fuck is going on," Brian shouts.

Jeremiah stands in front of me. I look over the side of his giant frame. "I'm sorry, Brian."

"Tell him it's over," Jeremiah says.

"How could you do this to me?" Brian says. The hurt look in his eyes breaks my heart.

"I'm sorry. I didn't mean for this to happen," I cry. I've never heard him yell so loud.

"The door is unlocked. I thought something happened to you, and you're fucking this man. What did you mean to happen? You're going to throw years down the drain for this clown."

The guilt is eating me alive. I didn't give my relationship another thought, and that's not like me. I've never cheated on Brian. Tears stream from my eyes.

"Who the fuck are you calling a clown?" Jeremiah says. "You're the only clown I see."

"You think you can come in here and fuck my girl?" Brian asks.

"She's not your girl."

"Please, stop," I yell.

"Shante, explain yourself," Brian yells, causing me to jump. "How long has this been going on?"

I begin to speak, but I don't have the words.

"Talk!" Brian yells.

Jeremiah replies. "She's done."

"I was talking to Shante," Brian says.

"Anything you have to say to her, you can say to me now."

"Is this how it is? You won't even talk to me?" Brian asks.

"I'm sorry," I say.

"One of my boys called me and swore you had a guy with you last night, and I said Shante wouldn't do that. She's a good one. I thought I knew you."

"You do. I made a mistake." I manage to maneuver around Jeremiah.

"No, I made the fucking mistake. I thought you were loyal."

"Brian," I cry, pleading.

"Now, I know you're nothing but a whore, just like your mother," Brian yells.

50

I can't believe he said that. He knows how to hit me where it hurts most. The last thing I want in this world is to end up like my mother.

Jeremiah punches Brian in the face. "You don't talk to her like that."

Brian wipes blood from his lips and laughs. "I'm not going to fight you for her. She's not worth it. You can keep her trifling ass." He storms out of the apartment.

The sound of the door slamming vibrates in my ears. I'm sure the whole complex heard this fiasco.

I drop to the floor, sobbing. Jeremiah kneels at my side and puts his arms around me.

"Don't touch me," I shout.

"Shante, you have nothing to feel bad about."

"How can you say that? This was the worst thing I could've done."

"I know it was hard, but it's over. We're going to be okay."

"Get your hands off me."

"Shante, baby."

"I'm not your baby. Did you see that? I hurt him. I threw away my relationship for someone I just met yesterday."

"You don't believe that."

"Brian and I have history. You don't know anything about us or what we've been through. He's not perfect, but I shouldn't have done that, and if you can't understand that, I don't know about you."

"Lower your voice. You're upset. You don't know what you're saying."

"I know what I'm saying. I'm a horrible person. Apparently, I'm a whore. If I had walked in and seen what he saw, I'd say the same thing."

"The circumstances are different. You and I belong together."

"We do? Do we? Why do we belong together, Jeremiah? Do you know what that sounds like? Would you

—

51

want to be with someone who did what I just did to Brian?"

"It's not that simple. I need you to calm down. I need to tell you something."

I try my best to speak calmly. "I don't want to hear it."

"Shante, listen to me," he shouts.

"No, you need to leave."

Jeremiah stands. "I'm not leaving you like this."

"I don't want you here. I don't want to see you."

"You don't mean that."

"I mean it. Why are you still here? I said, get out."

"If you let me explain, I can make all this make sense."

"You can't. This can't happen. It's over. We don't have anything. It was a stupid mistake. We got caught up in a moment. It was a crazy day. It wasn't real."

"I'm not leaving you."

"You have to. I don't want you. You're not even my type."

"Don't say something you'll regret just because you're hurt."

"You're arrogant, stuck up, and judgmental. Why would I want you? You're pushy and mean. It's because of you I'm in this fucked up position. I wish we never met. I could never love you. I don't want to be with you." Each word feels like I'm stabbing myself in the chest, and I can see his heart break with every syllable. Now I feel even worse about myself.

He rolls his neck around and clasps his hands. I expect him to yell and curse me out, but his voice is eerily calm. "Very well, Shante. I can't believe I was going to mate you. I fought it with everything in me, and now I know why."

"What the fuck are you talking about? What are you still doing here? Leave."

He begins to speak but opts to walk away instead.

My heart breaks. When the door closes, I melt into the floor. I want to tell him I was wrong, beg him to stay. I don't want to be alone, but I hate myself right now. How could anyone else love me? I don't deserve to be happy. I cry until there are no tears left. I stay in my spot on the floor for what feels like hours. I realize I still have Jeremiah's jacket wrapped around me. It smells like him. I just want to lay here in his scent. We were so close, but close to what, I'll never know.

VI ~ Jeremiah

In her final days, I listened to her stories as we sipped whiskey. She was a dear friend, the Nana I never had. She was quite a woman, and she'll be missed by many.

I chose to arrive late to the church and sit in the back. It takes no time for my wolf to scent Shante. Her hair is pulled back into a ponytail, and she's wearing all black as she sits on the front row next to some family members I recognize from the photos at Nana's house. I see their faces as they turn around and look at the crowd that showed up for their Nana. I guess I shouldn't be surprised I'm not the only wolf here. I can't imagine there's anyone who met Mable Ann Wilson that didn't love her.

Looking at the photos in the program I see why she had men chasing after her. She was a certified heartbreaker.

The missionaries are all dressed in white on the righthand side of the church. Nana was one of them. I laugh to myself as I look at their noses in the air and think of her saying they all had sticks up their asses.

Though I can sense emotion all around me, I feel Shante's pain like it's my own. I haven't seen her in about three months. She never came back to my class, and I

---

assume she stopped going to school. I kept myself buried in work, so I wouldn't think about her. Now that she's in the same room as me, every moment of our short time together floods my mind. I never want to think about that day again, but I'm forced to relive the pain. The words she spewed at me still sting. I try to push thoughts of her out of my mind, but how can I think about Nana without thinking about Shante?

I suffer through the endless number of songs, prayers, scripture readings, and remarks that are supposed to be limited to two minutes. I can't blame anyone for needing more time to remember Nana. They each have memories of a vibrant woman who loved life, and although I adore their stories, I find myself listening to Shante's breathing more than anything else.

I don't need a service to remember this great woman, but I promised her I'd be here for Shante. I told her I was done with her granddaughter, and there was nothing she or anyone else could do to make me change my mind. Only Nana would make it her dying wish that I take care of Shante during this difficult time.

"*She doesn't know it, but she's going to need you, and you're going to need her.*" I can hear her frail voice when she asked me for this one thing. I have a feeling she knew that would be the last time I saw her. How could I deny her this? I can't.

I follow the procession to the gravesite. Shante is holding it together well. I think Nana may have been wrong. She'll be fine.

"Earth to earth, ashes to ashes, and dust to dust." There's not a dry eye around when the minister says those words. This is the end. She's gone, and I'm holding back tears, but I have to keep it together for Nana and for Shante.

My eyes are glued to Shante as everyone moves around, hugging one another, greeting one another, asking who's going to the repass at Nana's house. I stand away from the crowd, watching. Shante stays seated, staring at the casket as her mother approaches her with open arms. I can smell the alcohol on her mom from here.

"I'm sorry, baby," her mother says over and over as she cries on Shante's shoulder.

Shante remains quiet.

"It's okay, Mom," Shante says.

It's not lost on me that Shante is the one comforting her mother and not the other way around. I want to step in and rescue her. Let her know I'm here for her, but she's handling herself well enough at this point.

Someone taps me on my shoulder. I turn around. "Mr. Jacobs," I say. "I saw you in the church. How are you, sir?"

Percy is as tall as me with brown skin and grey hair. "Call me Percy, son. I'm doing fine."

"How did you know Nana?" I ask.

"You might be too young for that story."

"I'd gotten to know Nana pretty well. Trust me, I can handle it."

"She and I were involved a long time ago. She was a little older than me, and I was head over heels for her. I didn't want to live without her, but then—"

"You met your mate." I finish his sentence. "That was you? She told me about you."

"Yep. We both went on to marry other people, but we always kept in touch. Mable was quite a woman."

"Indeed, she was," I say.

"I see you can't keep your eyes off the young lady in the front row," Percy says.

"It's her granddaughter, Shante."

"Why aren't you sitting next to her?" Percy asks.

"That's not my place," I say.

Percy studies me. I see the wheels turning in his mind. "Am I wrong to assume she's your mate?"

"Not anymore," I say.

Percy nods his head. "Not anymore, you say? How does that work exactly?"

"We lost touch. I haven't seen her in months."

56

"You thought distance and time would help you forget about your mate."

"I've managed, sir."

"How's that working out for you?"

"Just fine. I did my thing. I'm sure she did hers."

"That's interesting. My mate and I broke up for a week and I was beside myself. I was too stubborn to make things right, but my I felt terrible. My mind was messed up. I don't know how you've gone months."

"I'm in control of my emotions."

"What happened between you two, son?"

"We met one fateful night. She drove me crazy, and later that evening, I realized it was because—"

"Because you love her," Percy interrupts.

"I wasn't going to say that. Anyway, I got to know her and Mable. Everything seemed perfect, but the next morning, I went to her house, and her boyfriend showed up.

"She has a boyfriend?"

"She told me she was ready to break up with him. I told her to do it right away. If she had listened to me, things might be different. She asked me for one last kiss before she did it. It told her no, but she kept insisting. He walked in on us."

"Damn."

"Then she turned on me. She lashed out at me. She said some fu—, some messed up stuff to me. I was the guy that had spent my entire night making sure she was okay, the one who made sure she was safe when her so-called boyfriend left her stranded, the one who was about to risk it all to be with her. She ripped my heart out."

"Did she apologize?"

"I haven't heard from her since then, but it wouldn't have mattered."

"Life is precious, son. Do you want to make memories or live with regrets?"

"The memories I have aren't too pleasant, Percy. I'm not going there again."

57

"So, why are you here?"

"I made a promise to Nana, I mean, Mable. She's the only reason I'm here."

"You kids, I swear." Percy shakes his head. "When people say love isn't easy, you young people need to take heed. Love takes real commitment. The problems are real, but when it's love, especially with your mate, it's worth the effort. When are you kids going to learn? There are some things you can't run from." Percy places a comforting hand on my shoulder before he walks away. "I'll see you later, son."

I nod and take a deep breath. I think I should leave. I'm not sure where Shante's mother went, but Shante seems to be doing okay, and after rehashing what went down I don't know how much more I can take.

She rises from her seat and walks to the casket. Her hand grazes the lid. Her spirit is weary, and she's weak. Her knees buckle.

I run to catch her before she can hit the ground. I can only hope I didn't bring any unnecessary attention to myself because all I can think about is getting to her. I hold her up in my arms and press her into my chest. Tears stream like a river while she sobs. She wraps her arms around me. Her grasp isn't as strong as it once was. She's not okay.

I hope the warmth of my body brings her some comfort. "I'm here for you," I say as I kiss her forehead.

Her body stiffens. "Jeremiah," she whispers. "Is that you?"

"I'm here," I say.

She looks up. I know she's confused. I am too, but she buries her head in my chest and cries. "Jeremiah. You're here. You're here." She holds me as tight as she can.

I listen to her heartbeat. Holding her in my arms is a feeling I can't describe. I look up, and Percy is staring at us. He gives me a nod and a look that says I told you so before he walks off.

People begin to leave. Some come over to ask me if she's okay. I assure them she's fine, and I'll take care of her. I'll stand here with her as long as she needs me. I don't want to tell her it's going to be okay because it's not. I don't want to give her false promises. I want to be here, and that's what I continue to tell her. "I'm here for you."

Eventually, she loosens her grip. Most of her family and friends are gone. "Are you real?" She asks me.

"I'm real."

"How?"

"I didn't want you to go through this alone, and neither did Nana. I came in case you needed me."

She lays her head on my chest. "I do need you," she says.

"That's why I'm here."

"Jeremiah?"

"Yes, Shante."

"I can't go to Nana's house."

"I understand."

"I can't go home," she says.

"You don't have to."

"My Nana's not here anymore," she sobs. Her body feels weightless. I have to hold her up.

"I know. I'm so sorry," I say. I do my best to hold myself together. I have to be strong for Shante.

Once she's settled, I move her to the chair she used earlier.

"When was the last time you ate?"

"I don't know," she whispers.

"We're going to get you some food, okay?"

"I can't go to Nana's house, not right now."

"We can get you something else, but you need to eat."

"I'm not hungry."

"I know. Can you eat something light? For me?" I nod. She nods with me. "Okay," she says.

"Let's get out of here," I say.

"Okay."

"Can you stand?"

"Yes."

"My car is right over here," I say.

"You have a car?" she asks.

"Of course, I have a car." I help her to her feet.

She grabs my hand and intertwines her fingers with mine. The connection sends a burst of energy through my body that I try to resist with everything in me. I don't want to lose sight of what I'm doing here. I'm going to make sure she's okay. Then I'm done.

When we reach my car, I open the door for Shante, and she settles into the passenger seat.

"You ready?" I ask her as I start the car.

She lifts my armrest and scoots closer to me. My bicep presses against my shirt as she lays her head on my shoulder. I turn the radio to an easy listening station, and we drive to my house in silence.

"Shante, we're here."

She looks up. "Where are we?"

"My house."

"You live in the woods?" she asks.

"Near the woods," I say. "If it's a problem, I can take you somewhere else. Anywhere you want to go."

"No, this is good. Your home is beautiful." She sits up.

I can't help but think about how it could've been ours. "Thank you." I get out and open her door. "Welcome, Madame." I bow as she exits the car. I'm pleased when she smiles at me.

"Thank you, kind sir," she says.

"Wow. This is gorgeous," she says as we step inside.

"Let me take your coat."

"Thank you."

I hang her coat and mine in the closet by the door. "Make yourself at home. Can I get you anything?"

"No."

I walk her to the couch. "Have a seat."

She sits and stares into space. I turn the television to an action movie. Hopefully, this is something that won't remind her of Nana.

—
60

"I'll be right back," I say.

I run up the stairs to change and grab a blanket and a t-shirt. "Get comfortable. I'm going to get you some food. You can change into this if you'd like."

I cook her dinner and bring two plates to the table along with some wine. She walks into the dining room wearing my shirt. I try to stop my arousal at the sight of her thighs. She grabs a glass of wine as she sits at the table. "I can't believe you cooked for me."

"It's the least I could do."

"Steak and potatoes? This isn't light."

"You'll feel better when you eat a hardy meal, and we're not getting up from this table until you're done."

"I don't have to do what you say."

"My house, my rules."

She chuckles. "You sound like my Nana."

"I can imagine," I smile. "You know she'd want you to eat."

She nods her head as she holds back tears.

"It's okay to cry. Let it all out. Come here." I sit her on my lap. She wraps her arm around my neck and lays her head on my shoulder. I cut her steak into small pieces and feed her.

She eats slowly, barely chewing, until she gets some food in her belly. I feel her regaining strength, and I'm relieved. She sits up and drinks some wine. "You're an excellent cook," she says. After a few more bites, she grabs the fork from my hand.

"Maybe you're just hungry," I say.

Before I know it, she's cleaned her plate.

"Do you want some of mine?" I ask.

"No, I couldn't."

"It's fine. I have more, and you need to eat."

"Thank you," she says as she grabs my plate.

"Damn, girl. Don't forget to chew."

Her eyes widen, and she covers her mouth with her hand. "What?"

"You're inhaling that shit."

—

She pushes my shoulder and tries to yell, but food starts flying out of her mouth.

"Can't even keep your food in your mouth. That don't make no damn sense."

"Don't be mean," she says.

"I'm telling it like it is. I'm embarrassed for you."

"I can't believe you," she yells. She starts laughing, that contagious laugh of hers.

I breathe a sigh of relief. I know it won't last long, but I'm glad I made her laugh. "I can't believe you," I say.

"Jeremiah, I will smash these potatoes in your face."

"No, you won't."

"Don't call my bluff. I'll do it."

"Shante, don't you put those potatoes on my face. I'm not playing."

"You sound scared."

"I'm not scared. I know you're not crazy."

She picks up some potato and holds it to my face. "Say, I won't."

I look her in her eyes, her big beautiful eyes. "You won't," I say.

She moves it closer. "Say, I won't."

I grab her wrist. "You know you don't want to do that," I say.

"I might," she says.

We struggle back and forth, laughing until the mood shifts, and we're staring into one another's eyes. Shante eats the potato, and I smile. She touches my cheek. The magnetic pull between us is strong.

I clear my throat. "I was going to get some wood for the fireplace. Why don't you finish eating, and I'll be right back?"

"That sounds good," she says.

I take a deep breath when I walk away from the table. That was close. She almost sucked me in. I need to relieve some stress. I go to the back of the house and take my clothes off. The aggression and tension are too much for me. My wolf needs to break free. I shift as I jump over the

---

fence and take off into the woods. This is what I need, to feel the wind in my fur and the dirt underneath my paws.

The relief is sweet, but not sweet enough. I have to get back before Shante starts looking for me. I take in the air, and the smell of deer overtakes me. I follow the scent. I can't fight the urge to hunt.

My wolf craves its savory taste, and since he can't have what he really wants, he can have the animal. I stalk behind a bush and wait. The deer takes off running at the sound of my mighty growl. I smell his fear as I chase him down. He's fast, and this challenge is exactly what I need.

I'm on his heels, waiting for my moment to pounce.

He looks back, and I growl as I push from my hind legs and crash into his side. He struggles as I sink my claws and canines into his flank. The sweet taste of blood soothes me. He fights hard, wildly kicking his legs, crying in agony as I tear into his flesh until I've overpowered him, and his body goes limp. I feast on his meat. I howl once I'm full. My wolf is settled enough for me to head back home after I wash my face in a nearby stream. My mind is clear. I peek over the fence. No sign of Shante. I hop over the fence and put my sweatpants on. Then, I make quick work of chopping some wood and bring it inside.

Shante is sitting in front of the television. "Hey, you were gone for a while."

"Sorry about that."

"What happened to your shirt?"

I look down. "I took it off."

"Weren't you cold?" she asks.

"Chopping wood warms me up."

"Oh. I wish I was there to see that."

"No, you don't."

"I didn't know it was so much trouble. You got something in your hair. Did you get dirt on your face?"

She sure is full of observations, all of a sudden. I'm beginning to feel uncomfortable. "Yeah, I'm going to take a shower before I light the fire. You okay?" I try to stay as far away as possible.

"I'm fine. I have my wine to keep me company."

"I'll be right back."

I head up the stairs and look in the mirror. I should've been more careful. I can't have any more incidents like that while she's here.

The warmth of the shower as the water streams down my fade allows me to relax, but now, I'm in need of a different kind of release. My dick is rock hard, and I can't go back like this. I don't need the temptation. I take it in my hands and attempt to soothe the problem. *Just think about anything other than Shante*, I tell myself. Of course, she's all I can think about, so I give in.

I bite my bottom lip. All I can think about is being inside her, an experience I never had. I think about her pussy. I had only touched it briefly so I have to use my imagination. I remember the warmth between her legs. I remember how wet she was for me, the way her moisture coated my fingers and I had barely touched her. I imagine what it must be like to be inside her. I lean my head against the wall and hold back moans as I stroke myself, hard and fast. I'm lost in the moment until the sound of my name snaps me out of my trance.

"Jeremiah," Shante says.

I open my eyes. "What the fuck, Shante?" I shout.

VII ~ Shante

"Damn," I say, ignoring his question. I can't focus on anything he's saying. I knew he had a big dick, but seeing it in all its glory is something I'll never forget. You could hang a shower curtain on that thing. I've been fighting these urges since he held me in his arms at the funeral. I want him. I step closer to his shower. I need to see it up close.

"Shante, what are you doing?" he asks.

"I don't know. I forgot."

"Well, can I have some privacy?"

"No, I don't think so. Please continue," I say.

He's still holding himself, and he's still hard. "Shante, quit playing."

"Let me see."

"Get out of here now." His serious expression only makes me want him more.

We have a staring match. It becomes obvious that I'm not going to budge. He gives in and furiously strokes his dick.

I gasp while he grunts.

"What are you doing?" I ask. I lick my lips, grateful to whoever invented the shower with the glass door.

"I'm in my shower minding my own damn business. What the hell are you doing in here?" His head rolls back and his eyes close.

"I could help you with that."

"That's not for you to enjoy."

"Well, someone should. Why not me?"

He breaths quicken. And he growls. He's close. I know it. He holds his dick straight up, and I can see the cum oozing over the head before it's washed away by the water. I've never been much of a swallower, but I want to taste every drop of him. I want to get on my knees on the shower floor and take him in my mouth, all of him. His eyes close, and he shakes his dick and lays his head against the wall.

I step closer.

He takes a deep breath and washes his body in a hurry. When he rinses off, the water cascades over his skin like a waterfall. It's the sexiest thing I've ever seen in my life.

I grab a towel and head toward the shower. "Here you go," I say.

He steps out and picks me up along with the towel.

I scream while he tickles me and carries me into his room.

"Jeremiah, stop," I yell.

"What are you doing watching me?"

"I couldn't tear my eyes away."

"Try," he says.

He lifts me and throws me down onto his bed. I am so turned on, I can't function. He climbs in next to me. This bed is huge and it's comfortable. I feel like I'm on a cloud. His sheets are black, which I find extremely sexy. I rest on my elbows, thinking this is it. He's going to give me the Moby dick, and I'm going to let him. He snatches his towel before he gets out of bed and walks away.

I curse while I lay back and sink into the comfort of his comforter. I've never had a bed in the bag like this. I wonder where people with money buy their linens.

—

Never before has any man consumed my mind like Jeremiah. Not a day has gone by that I haven't thought of him. I said some pretty awful things that I can never take back. I couldn't bring myself to face him after that. The fact that he's even talking to me is a miracle. I don't know where he came from, but I'm grateful he's here. I want so badly to apologize, and to thank him for rescuing me again, but I don't know where to begin. I hope that him bringing me here means we can work something out.

There were moments when he made me laugh, but the pain in my heart is still there. His body was a nice distraction, though. I wonder if he thought about me while he was working that dick out.

I'm so lost in thought. I didn't even realize he'd left the room and come back. "Do you want to sit by the fire?" he asks.

I jump at the sound of his voice. "Why did you put on clothes?" I ask.

"Because I don't want to tempt you," he replies.

"Please, tempt me."

"Come on," he says.

"Can you carry me?"

He approaches the bed and lifts.

I wrap my legs around his waist and bury my head in his neck. He's not wearing any cologne. His natural scent is divine. I can't stop myself from pressing my lips against him.

He flinches, and I stiffen. I am so drawn to him. I forgot about the power he has over me. "How do you pick me up like I'm weightless?"

"That's my little secret."

"Your little secret is not so little," I say.

"Behave, Shante."

"Yes, sir."

He places me on the couch in front of the fireplace, and I curl up next to the arm. The feel of a warm blanket covers me. "I like this. I've never been in front of a real

___

67

fireplace." I listen to the fire crackling. He's quiet. Too quiet.

Images of Nana holding my hand as she passed away flood my mind. I'll never forget the look on her face or the moment she let go. My heart stopped. I try to hide my tears, but it doesn't work.

"It's alright." He sits next to me with his arms open.

"I can't do this without her. She's all I had."

"You'll always have her. She gave you everything you need." Jeremiah rubs my hair and rocks me like Nana used to.

"It's not the same."

"I know. Nothing could replace that woman, but you're just like her."

"I wish."

"You are. You're fierce and determined. You got that mouth of yours from her. You know that, don't you? You stand out. That's all courtesy of your grandmother."

"You want to hear something funny?" I ask.

"Yeah."

"I used to be super shy."

"I don't believe that for one second."

I chuckle. "When I first came to live with Nana, I hardly talked. I would stay in my room and keep to myself. When my cousins came over, I'd sit back and watch them play. I was the same way at school. You'd think she'd be happy I was staying out of trouble, but Nana wasn't having that."

"What happened?"

"One day, she came into my room and started going off. She said, 'Lil' girl, let me ask you something.' I jumped up. The sound of her voice made me think I did something wrong. She said, 'When I walk into the room, do I go hide in the corner?' I was like, 'no, ma'am'. She said, 'And neither should you'. I was so confused." I smile.

"That sounds like her," Jeremiah smiles.

68

"She said, 'You can't be scared to be who you are. People want to know you, the real you, so stop hiding. When you walk into the room, you let everybody know you're there, honey'." I roll my neck and shake my finger like she used to.

"Nana was something else," Jeremiah says.

"She was. She said, 'Who are you'? I said, 'Shante'. I was confused as hell. She said, 'I still don't know who you are. Say it like you mean it'. I said, 'Shante'. She said, 'Louder,' so I yelled, 'Shante'. She said, 'You are Shante Wilson, damnit, and don't you let anybody forget it. What's your name?' I said, 'Shante Wilson.' She said, 'That's not what I said'. I looked around like, *is she telling me I can cuss*. She said, 'Let me hear it, and I'm going to whoop your ass if you don't get it right'. I cleared my throat, and I yelled with all the sass I could muster, 'I'm Shante Wilson, damnit, and you better not forget it'. We laughed and laughed."

"That's hilarious," Jeremiah says.

"She helped me find myself. She helped me find my voice. Without her I wouldn't have known who I was. I used to watch her with her friends, at the store, or at church. She had a way with people. Everybody wanted to be around her. People tend to flock to her wherever she goes. I only hope I can be a portion of what she was."

"Are you kidding? You're all Nana. Don't ever forget that. Everything Nana had to offer is right here." He places his hand over my heart. The contact causes my pulse to race. *Does he feel it?*

I place my hand over his hand.

"Did you think about me?" I whisper.

He clears his throat and shuffles. "Can I get you anything? Some more wine?"

"Got anything stronger?"

"I have just the thing."

He gets up and brings back a bottle of whiskey and two glasses.

"Shut up. That was Nana's favorite."

—

"I know," he says. He sits next to me. "She made me bring her some whenever I came by. She said she was already dying, and a sip of whiskey wouldn't hurt."

"That sounds like her." I shake my head. "I hate this shit."

"Let's have one for Nana."

"Absolutely."

He pours two glasses. I sip mine while he drinks his in one gulp.

"So, you were really visiting Nana?" I ask.

"We became friends."

"She always asked about you. I guess she was pretending she hadn't seen you."

"I saw her quite a bit," Jeremiah says.

"What did you two talk about?" I ask.

"She told me stories about her life. She asked me about work. She talked about you. She loved you, and she was proud of the way you put your life together, considering everything you've been through. I told her she raised a hell of a lady."

"You don't have to be so nice to me. I don't deserve it."

"You deserve it."

"You just feel sorry for me."

He places a hand on my shoulder. "That's true."

I can't help but laugh.

We drink and laugh and talk about Nana. This is what I needed. Somehow, he knew.

"I don't know how you made such an impact on her. You two only met briefly," I say to Jeremiah.

"I was lucky. I guess she just liked me."

"That, I can understand." I smile at him. "You're pretty special."

"Can I get you anything?" he asks.

"Jeremiah, I'm fine. You've helped me more than you'll ever know. I'm so sorry I took up your whole Saturday."

"Don't apologize. I wanted to be here for you. I mean that."

"I don't know how I'll ever repay you, and not just for today. I owe you a lot."

"It's fine. I sent your bill in the mail."

"Stop making jokes. You're a good man. I know it." I caress his cheek, and he doesn't pull back.

"Thank you," he says.

"There are so many things I want to say to you. I just—" My voice trails off.

"You don't have to say anything." He touches my hand.

"Maybe you're right." I stand over him while he watches my every movement. My lips can't resist his. I kiss him.

He's hesitant at first, but it only takes a moment for him to kiss me back. I've missed this feeling, the warmth of his soft lips. I don't know how I could've lived without his kiss or his touch these last few months. We pull apart, and he stands. I get excited about the thought of him carrying me back to his bed.

"You must be tired. It's late," he says.

"I'm not tired."

"You need to get some sleep."

"Oh. Sure," I guess I'm about to go to sleep, because he's not really giving me a choice.

He leads me up the stairs. "Behind door number one, we have a spacious room with a large TV."

It's across the hall from his room. I step inside. "I'll take it," I say.

"Are you sure you don't want door number two?"

"Is door number two your bedroom?"

"No."

"Well, I'll settle for door number one."

"Okay. You have your own bathroom, so you don't have to come into mine."

"I'm going to pretend I didn't hear that."

71

"If you get hungry or need anything, please, make yourself at home."

"Thanks."

"Goodnight, Shante."

"Goodnight."

I spend the night tossing and turning. The pain of Nana's funeral, and thoughts of Jeremiah, consume me. I know I'm pushing it, and he's already done enough, but I need to be close to him.

I find myself standing outside his room. Do I really want to do this? I do. My knuckles lightly touch the door. He doesn't reply, so I turn the knob and push the door ajar. He doesn't tell me to stop, so I walk in and crawl in bed next to him. I snuggle against his naked body. He puts his arm around me and holds me tight. I feel his breath on my neck. Damn, this feels good. His body is so warm. I adjust my body so his dick is accidentally perfectly positioned against my ass.

"I couldn't sleep," I say.

"Me either. I don't think it's a good idea for you to be in here."

"It feels like a good idea." I'm referring to his dick expanding.

"That's the problem."

"It's not a problem. I won't stay long. Please don't make me leave."

"You can stay for a little while."

"Thank you."

"Go to sleep," he says.

"Don't tell me what to do," I say.

"Don't argue with me."

"I will argue with you till I'm blue in the face."

"Of course, you will."

"What are you going to do about it?"

He releases me from his hold. That's the worst thing he can do right now. I lay there cold, wondering if I can tell him to hold me again when something knocks me in the head.

—

72

"Ahhh," I yell. "You hit me with a pillow." I cover my face as he hits me over and over again. I can't help but giggle. My body twists and contorts with every blow. "Stop."

"Don't try to cover yourself now," he says. "I thought you were talking shit?"

"I can back it up."

He hits me again. "Yeah, right." He swings again but misses when I roll over and lunge for a pillow.

"That's right," I say as I rise to my knees. I swing my pillow and aim for his head. "You're going down," I say as I unsuccessfully dodge his pillow. I get some hits in, though.

"Not today," he says. He rises to his knees, and I remember he's naked.

I try not to think about his body, so I knock him from side to side with my pillow. He swings at my head. "That's the last straw," I say.

"What are you going to do?" he asks.

I wind up my arm and spin my pillow like helicopter propellers. Then, I swing as hard as I can at his torso. "Got you."

"Ahhh," he yells. His body caves over as he writhes in pain. I turn on the lamp next to his bed. His facial expression is strained.

He can't be serious. "Jeremiah, what's wrong?"

He holds his side and rocks back and forth, making agonizing faces.

"I'm so sorry. What should I do? Are you hurt?" I try to touch him, but I'm scared.

"Ahhh," he yells.

"I'm so sorry, Jeremiah. Hold on. I'll call 911."

"No," he yells while he squirms.

"I have to. You're hurt."

His body straightens, his eyes open wide, and he erupts into laughter.

"What?" My confusion makes it difficult for my brain to catch up to my eyes. I give him a once over before I

73

make the connection. "You asshole. I can't believe you did that. What's wrong with you?"

He keeps laughing. I love to see him laugh. He's usually serious, but he's laughing at me, and for that, he must die. "Jeremiah, what's wrong?" He mocks me.

I swing at his chest and hit him repeatedly. He grabs my hands and holds them as he lays beneath me. My breathing becomes heavy as I look into his eyes.

We freeze.

I rip my hands from his grip and turn my back to him. My arms are folded across my chest. "I can't believe you did that to me," I yell. "You're so fucking disrespectful. You do that right after my grandmother dies. I thought something happened to you." I make crying noises.

I feel him jump up. He places a hand on my shoulder. "I'm sorry. I wasn't thinking."

I pull my shoulder from his grip. "I don't care."

"Shante, I would never do that to you. It was stupid. I was just playing with you." He wraps me in his arms.

I squirm and manage to turn to face him. The worry in his eyes is priceless. "Gotcha," I say.

"That's some cold-blooded shit," he yells.

I roll over laughing.

"That's enough. Take your ass to bed," he says.

"Somebody can dish it, but they can't take it," I laugh.

"Take this." He hits me with a pillow.

I yell.

He pounces on top of me and tickles me relentlessly. I try to escape, but he's powerful. "I give up," I say.

"What was that? I couldn't hear you." He continues to tickle me.

"I give up," I repeat over and over.

"You sure?"

"Yes. You win."

"Say, yes, Big Daddy."

"Yes, Big Daddy."

Say it like you mean it.

"Yes, Big Daddy."

"Okay." He stops and lays next to me. He takes a deep breath and stretches.

I take the opportunity to tickle him, but he doesn't move at all. I look at him. He has an annoying smirk. I tickle again. Nothing. "What's wrong with you?" I ask.

"I'm not ticklish."

"That's not possible. Everybody is ticklish."

"Not me."

I rise to my knees and poke him.

He grabs my hand. "That's not nice."

I give him light tickles, and he smiles.

"You may as well give up."

"Never," I say. "It's a modern miracle." I stare at his body. His dick is erect as he lays there like he doesn't notice. I'm not ignoring this thing anymore.

"Let's go to bed," he says.

"I have a better idea. Let's see what you can feel." I graze his neck with the tips of my fingers.

He shivers.

"You felt that?"

"Yeah," he says.

In the same manner, I run my fingertips down his arm and watch him.

His eyes close.

I do the same on his chest.

He licks his lips.

I thought I'd never see him again. I've wanted him for so long, and he's here in front of me. I wonder if he still wants me. If only I had the courage to tell him how I feel.

I flick his nipples with my fingers. His hips lift, and he takes a deep breath.

"Shante, I think you should go back to your room."

"I'm trying to see something." My hand travels lower. I trace his muscular abs. I grab his hardened length in my hand and pump up and down.

"Shante," he whispers.

"Shhh." I watch his dick get harder, and excitement drips between my legs. I swirl my tongue around his tip.

—

75

I know he's concentrating on resisting pleasure. I can see it in his strained face. That only turns me on more.

"Can you feel this, Jeremiah?" I take the head into my mouth and suck.

He moans.

"You feel that, don't you, Big Daddy?" I suck up and down his length while my hand works his base.

"Shante," he whispers.

"Say my name again."

"Shante."

"Just like that."

"Shante, we have to stop," he pleads. His fingers grip my hair. I worry he's going to push me away, but he struggles with pulling my head down further.

I brace myself and take his whole length in my mouth. I can feel his head in my throat. I take it all in, covering him with my mouth and relaxing my throat. I bob my head.

His hips lift off the bed. Saliva oozes from my mouth, and I lose myself, sucking and slurping. I lick the sides and take his balls into my mouth. Pleasure and agony are written on his sexy face.

I get lost in the salty taste of his tip. My head moves up and down and side to side, focusing on his pleasure and mine. I love this dick, the texture, the taste, the massive length, the girth. I've never sucked a dick with this much enthusiasm.

I lift my head. "I've thought about you every day for the past two months. I've missed you so much," I say.

"Three," he says.

"What was that?" I ask.

"It's been three months since I've seen you."

He has been thinking about me. "I guess you're right."

"We can't do this," he says.

I kiss my way up his body. "I need you, Jeremiah. Please don't turn me away. I need you to take the pain away. Please. I never thought I'd have this chance, but

—

76

we're here, and I don't want to lose this moment." I look in his eyes.

He touches my cheek. I kiss his palm and up his arm. I reach his lips, and I'm excited when he doesn't fight my kiss. I can't stop the tears from flowing when he kisses me back. Our tongues complement one another perfectly as I straddle his giant body. He grabs my hips and sinks his fingers into my skin.

I lift myself and remove his shirt from my body. He wipes my tears with his thumbs. "This is too much for you. We should stop."

"It's not."

"Then why are you crying?"

"I haven't been happy since the moment I told you to leave. I felt like I lost a piece of myself, and now you're here and—" I shrug.

"Shante, let's talk," he says.

"I don't want to talk."

"You're not thinking clearly."

"Make love to me."

"Shante, you're talking crazy. I'm trying my hardest to be a gentleman."

"I don't want you to be a gentleman."

"I should."

"Jeremiah, what the fuck is wrong with you? Why do I have to convince you to do what you clearly want to do? Your dick knows what it wants. What's your problem? Stop acting like—"

Before I know it, I'm on my back, and he has my arms and legs pinned to the bed. I can't move.

He growls, but not like before. It comes from deep within him.

I gasp. "Do that again," I say.

"Shante, I've wanted to tell you something since the day we met."

"What's that?"

"Shut the fuck up."

77

Before I can react, his head dives between my legs, and he growls with his tongue pressed against my clit. My body vibrates, and I cry out. My legs tremble as his tongue explores my heat. Bursts of pleasure explode as he devours me like no man ever has.

"Jeremiah. That feels so good."

His tongue is fast and precise. I lift my hips and squeeze his face between my thighs. I grasp his head and pull, rocking my hips against his face. "Take this pussy. It's yours." A wave of pleasure crashes over me. I cry out as he growls and sucks my clit. My body convulses, and I cover my face with my hands. My breaths are heavy, my cries desperate. The endless pleasure still courses through my body.

Jeremiah kisses his way up, biting me as he swirls his tongue along my body. He takes my breast into his mouth and sucks. I wrap my legs around him as he kisses my neck and then my lips. Our kiss is hungry, insatiable. Neither of us can get enough. We crave one another.

I reach my hand between our bodies and grab his dick. I rub the head against my entrance. I'm so wet I can hear the slurp of his dick soaking up my juices. The smoothness of his head pressed against my entrance makes me want to lose control. My eyes close. Electricity courses through my body as he takes charge, replacing my hand with his. He enters me slowly and kisses me while my body adjusts inch by inch to his girth.

"Damn, Big Daddy," I say as he fills me, stretches me, and solidifies his ownership of my body.

He growls as the force of his body slams into mine. He's in me so deep. His hips move at a perfect rhythm, in and out and in circles as he gives me everything I've been missing, everything I've ever needed.

"Mine," he whispers in my ear.

I wrap my legs around him and hold on tight. He pins my arms above my head and holds my leg in the air. His speed increases, but he remains very much in control as I cry out with each thrust. I can't help but scream his name

—

over and over. I'm losing my mind, and my legs are shaking. Another mind-blowing orgasm approaches. I hold onto his shoulders, screaming. His body moves faster than I ever thought was humanly possible. I hear his hips slapping against mine. My hips thrust to meet his, but I can barely keep up. I yell as pleasure explodes, and my mind goes numb. I buck wildly. He slows down as I come down, teasing my body. It takes time for me to catch my breath.

He pulls out and flips me over. I moan with anticipation as I lay flat on my stomach. Electric sensations flow through me as he enters me from behind. He takes his time exploring my body. His lips kiss my neck.

I lift my ass to meet his powerful thrusts.

"You feel so good, baby," he whispers in my ear.

All I can do is moan. Our bodies are one. This feels so good, so right. The way he touches me. The way he runs his fingers through my hair. The way he moans and digs his fingers into my skin. He enjoys every part of my body. I find it hard to believe he's ever made love to anyone else like this before. He pushes my leg forward and bends my knee. He holds onto my ass and I know he's lost himself in my body. A connection like ours can't be denied.

"Oh shit," I yell. I'm about to come. I cry out in ecstasy. "Jeremiah," I sing his name, and he goes wild. He growls as he pounds into me. He pulls out, tearing himself away, and grunts. I feel streams of his warmth pouring over my ass. He rubs his dick between my cheeks and kisses me on my neck.

As his body flops over onto his back, he stares at the ceiling. Moments later, he gets up and comes back with a warm towel. I can barely move. I'm grateful when he wipes me down. Neither of us says a word.

He holds me close as we drift off to sleep. Finally, I'm happy again.

Sometime later, I open my eyes, and he's still holding me tight. I smile to myself and run my finger across his arm. "I love you," I whisper. I kiss his hand and go back to sleep.

I awaken in Jeremiah's big, empty bed to the smell of bacon. He's cooking for me. That's so romantic. I go downstairs, and he sits a plate on the counter. He's dressed. I guess I'll have to take those clothes off him.

"Good morning," I say as I wrap my arms around his waist.

Jeremiah stiffens. "Good morning. I made you breakfast. Do you want to get dressed before we go?"

"I can get dressed after," I reply.

"Suit yourself. Have a seat." He places a plate in front of me. "Would you like some orange juice?"

"Sure. Are you going to eat?"

"I'm not hungry," he says.

"Really. I thought you would've worked up quite an appetite after last night." I grin from ear to ear.

"I ate a little something already. So, listen. We need to talk about last night."

"What's there to talk about?" I dig into the bacon and eggs he sat in front of me.

"I want to make sure we're on the same page."

"I'm pretty sure we are," I say.

"Oh, good. I mean, we were caught up in the moment and the grief, and I'm relieved we understand it was a one-time thing. I mean, I don't even know what your situation is, and I'm sure neither of us is looking for anything serious. The timing is just off."

My stomach drops, and so does my fork. "Right," I say. I take a sip of juice. I can barely get it down my throat. My appetite is gone along with my smile.

"So, I should take you home."

"No, no, don't worry, my ride is ten minutes away. I already booked it. I'll get dressed and wait outside. Thanks for everything." I gather my clothes, purse, and phone and book the quickest car that can get to me as I head out the door without so much as a glance in his direction. He

—

doesn't have to worry about me anymore. I want nothing form him.

His behavior was cold and distant. I feel like the world's biggest idiot. I thought what we shared was special, beautiful, life-changing. There's still some time for him to come to his senses. I look behind me to see if he comes after me, but deep down, I know he won't. I saw it in his eyes. I read this all wrong.

VIII ~ Jeremiah

Enough time has passed. I'd like to say it gets easier, but I'm not sure. I'd like to say I barely think about her, and that's true most of the time, but her scent lingers in my memory. Her laugh replays in my mind. Her pussy was made for me. My wolf doesn't want to let her go, but I do. I've made it clear that we're done with Shante, so he'll have to get over it. There's a longing I can't get rid of. Still, the anger remains. The words she said to me are imprinted in my brain. I don't want her, and I don't want to think about her. I was such a fool to consider mating her, to give my heart to her so easily, but I'll never be a fool again.

It's the first day of a new semester, and I have a new class to teach. I arrive at my classroom thirty minutes early and am rendered speechless.

"Hello, professor," she says as I walk through the door.

"What are you doing here?" I ask.

"I'm taking Civil Litigation this semester."

"Why?"

"Haven't you heard? I want to be the next Erin Brockovich."

I scoff. I'm not going to engage her. I take a seat at my desk and pull some papers from my briefcase.

"Nice sweater, professor."

I pretend to check the papers, but I'm really looking at my black button-down sweater. I know she's being sarcastic, but it is a nice sweater.

She comes to my desk. I don't bother looking up. "You can take a seat, Miss Wilson, or you have time to leave and come back if you'd like." I curse myself for not knowing she'd be in my class.

"Miss Wilson? Really Jeremiah? You've seen me naked, every part of my body."

The papers fall from my hands, and I quickly recover them.

"I need to talk to you," she says.

"I'll go over everything you need to know during class."

"Not about class."

"There's nothing else to talk about, Miss Wilson."

"Can you at least look at me, Jeremiah?"

I open a textbook and read the same line four times in a row.

"I wanted to say, thank you."

"There's no need."

"Yes, there is. You came to Nana's funeral."

"I wanted to keep a promise I made."

"But you didn't have to. You didn't have to be there for me either, but you were."

I take a deep breath. "I did what Nana wanted. That's all."

"You know it was more than that," she says. "You were there for me."

"I need to prepare for class, so if you'll take your seat."

"I understand why you're still mad at me. I never had a chance or the courage to say I'm sorry."

"There's no reason to apologize."

"There is. You and I both know it. Listen, that day was difficult for me."

"It was a long time ago. It was a mistake. I should've never come to your home or involved myself in your life. It was unprofessional. Enough time has passed for us to move on."

"You don't mean that."

"How's Brian?"

"Brian and I weren't right for one another."

I clear my throat. "I'm sorry to hear that. I'm sure you two can work it out. You seemed very much in love," I say.

"You know that's not true."

"I don't know anything. I know I was yelled at and kicked out after you were all over me, but it's fine. I've forgotten about it."

"It sounds like it."

"If that's all, I'm trying to prepare myself to teach."

"I didn't want Brian then and I don't want him now. There was nothing between us after he walked out of my door. The only man I've wanted since we met is you."

"You don't have to explain anything to me."

"I wanted to know if we could get to know one another."

"All you need to know about me is that you should address me as Professor Johnson, and anything you need to talk to me about should be related to Civil Litigation. I will go over all requirements once class begins."

"Jeremiah," she says.

"Professor Johnson," I remind her.

"You're really going to treat me this way."

"This is how I treat all my students."

"Jeremiah."

"I'm not going to tell you again to call me, Professor Johnson. If that's too hard for you, we may need to find you another class. I'd be happy to speak to your advisor or the dean."

"Why are you being so cold? You have to understand—"

Another student walks through the door. Her perfume hits my nose. She's wearing red lipstick, tight black pants, and I can scent her desire.

"Good evening, Professor Johnson," she says.

"Good evening, Amber," I say with a smile. Amber was in my class last semester. She was a good student, but I could tell she was interested in more than classwork.

"I'm excited to take another one of your classes. I enjoyed last semester. I know there's a lot more I need to learn about you," she catches herself, "I mean, from you."

"It's good to see you again. Class will begin shortly," I say.

Shante gives me a death stare. "Hello," she says to Amber.

Amber gives Shante a not so polite nod.

"I said, hello, Amber," Shante puts some attitude behind her voice.

"I'm sorry. Do I know you?" Amber asks.

"No, but you should. I'm Shante."

"That's nice," Amber says as she turns her attention back to me.

I can feel Shante's anger rising, and I must admit it's satisfying.

"Thanks, professor," Amber says. She walks away.

"I need to talk to you," Shante says.

"Let's see if I can answer your questions during class, Miss Wilson."

Shante nods and walks away before pausing and looking back at me. "Yes, Professor Johnson."

I turn my attention back to my textbook. Students trickle into the classroom a few at a time.

Once six o'clock comes, I address the class. "Welcome to Civil Litigation. I am Professor Johnson, and that's how you all will address me. Class begins at six pm. No one will be allowed in the classroom after six, so make sure to get here on time. Let's see who we have here." I check attendance. All students are present. I recognize a lot of them from previous classes, but there are a few new faces.

I grab a stack of papers from my desk and hand the first person on each row enough for their row. Shante sits in the front row, hanging on my every word. "This is your syllabus. Everything you need to know is here. All assignments must be turned in on time, with a cover sheet, and correctly formatted. There will be no exceptions. If it's not formatted correctly, it does not exist, and you will receive a failing grade. When you take Legal Research, you'll learn the importance of submitting documents correctly and free of error. My office hours are listed along with my email. Assignments are listed on the syllabus as well as projects. Does anyone have any questions?"

Shante raises her hand.

I nod my head to recognize her, even though I wish she weren't here.

"What happens if we're late to class?" Shante asks.

"Capital punishment," I say.

The class laughs.

"I guess I'd better be on my best behavior," Shante says.

"Any other questions?"

Amber raises her hand.

I nod. "Yes."

"Can we get extra credit?"

"I don't give extra credit. Anyone else?"

No one raises their hand.

"Let's get started with the differences between civil and criminal law. Who can tell me, in their own words, what criminal law is?"

Amber raises her hand.

"Yes, Amber," I say.

Amber begins to speak, but Shante interrupts. "Criminal law defines criminal activity and the punishment for said activity."

"That's fine, but let's try it without using the word in the definition."

"Okay, criminal law defines illegal activity and the punishment for said activity," Shante says.

"And who is the defendant in a criminal case?" I ask.

"The person who committed the crime," Shante says.

"Who is the plaintiff?"

"The state or government," Shante says.

"What is burden of proof?"

Amber raises her hand.

"Yes, Amber."

"Burden of proof refers to who's responsible for proving what they are claiming," Shante says.

"Very good, Shante."

"Professor, I had my hand raised," Amber says.

"This isn't Kindergarten. You don't have to raise your hand."

"But, you called on me."

"And, you let someone else answer. Is that my fault?"

"No, Professor Johnson," Amber says.

Shante looks satisfied.

"However, Shante," I address her.

"Yes, Professor Johnson?" She smiles, I assume she anticipates of some sort of praise.

"Let's give the other students a chance to speak."

"We all have the same chance, Professor Johnson," Shante says.

Her response makes my dick stiff. It sounds like something I would've said in law school. I worked twice as hard and was determined to be the best. I wasn't going to let anyone outdo me. I'm impressed with Shante, but I don't want her to know that, so I ignore her statement and move on. I don't know what kind of student she would've been last semester. Everything blew up so fast, and she never came back to class, but I'd bet good money she wouldn't have been the student in the front row, answering all the questions. I wonder what other surprises she has in store.

"Amber, where does the burden of proof lie in a criminal case?"

"The prosecution is responsible for proving the guilt of the defendant beyond a reasonable doubt."

"Very good, Amber. Reasonable doubt is the standard of proof in criminal cases, but we're not going to dwell on criminal law in this class because this is Civil Lit. The important thing is that you all know the differences between civil and criminal law. These differences will be on your first test. Let's talk about civil law." I remember a name I called from the attendance sheet. "Marie, can you tell me what civil law refers to?"

I can tell who Marie is because she's startled at the mention of her name.

"Me?" she asks.

"Is there another Marie here?" I ask.

"Ummm, I guess I would say it's stuff like cases where people have a problem with another person."

"Thank you, Marie. Civil law deals with disputes between individuals, between organizations, or between individuals and organizations. In civil cases, the plaintiff is seeking damages. What are damages?"

"Usually, a monetary reward."

"Very good, Shante."

"Does anybody know where the burden of proof lies in a civil case?"

"The plaintiff, who is the person who brought the case, is responsible for proving their case based on a preponderance of evidence," Shante speaks out.

"I see some confused faces, and that's fine. This was a brief intro to what we'll be discussing next class. I want you all to read chapter one of your textbooks. I find that students understand information better when we can have open discussions. I want you to be able to define criminal and civil law."

I look around the room.

"You should be writing this down." I pause to let the students write. "Define burden of proof and standard of proof, and tell me how they're different. Define plaintiff and defendant, and tell me who's the plaintiff and defendant in civil cases. Learn the definitions in chapter one and answer the review questions. If you have questions or need clarification about something you're reading, make a note. I'm here to make sure you understand the information, so don't hesitate to ask. That's all for this class. I'm going to let you all go early tonight, and I'll see you on Wednesday. Any questions, please see me after class. Goodnight."

Students file out of the class one by one. As I could've guessed, there are two students left. Shante sits in her chair while Amber heads to the front of the class as I sit at my desk.

"Thank you, professor. Would you recommend any books in addition to the textbook?"

I'm amused at the sight of Shante rolling her eyes at Amber's question.

"No, Amber, the textbook is fine for now."

"Well, I was wondering if you could sign this for me anyway." Amber pulls out a copy of my book, The Letter of the Law.

"You read my book?" I ask. I'm pleased. Shante is annoyed. I grab Amber's book and a sharpie from my briefcase, and I sign it.

"I enjoyed it very much. Maybe we can discuss it sometime after class," she says.

I change the subject. "I appreciate your dedication," I say.

"Okay, see you next class, Professor Johnson."

"Goodnight, Amber."

"I read your book too. Do I get a smile?"

"What can I do for you, Miss Wilson?" I ask as Amber leaves the room.

Shante doesn't speak until Amber is gone. "You can look at me."

I sigh and look at her. "Happy?"

"No," she says.

"What do you want?"

"I want to talk. Will you please talk to me?"

"We're talking."

"Allow me the opportunity to say what I need to say. Can you at least do that?"

"Fine, let's get this over with."

"Jeremiah," she begins.

I shake my head because she refuses to address me correctly.

She continues. "I owe you so much. First, a thank you. I owe you many thank yous, actually. I believe you came into my life for a reason, and you showed me what I've been missing. You were there for me when I wanted to give up. You don't know it, but you inspired me to be better, and I'm grateful."

"It's not a problem," I say as I gather my things.

She walks to my desk. "I owe you an apology," she says.

I sigh. I don't want to think about what happened between us. I only want to move on. "There's no need."

"You have to know I didn't mean the things I said that day. I felt bad about myself, not about you. The situation became too intense for me, and I lashed out at you because you were there. You didn't deserve that at all, and I'm sorry. You've only ever tried to help me. You've only tried to show me how a man should treat a woman."

"It's fine," I say.

"It's not. There's no good excuse for how I acted. I'm sorry." She bows her head and her voice softens. "I'd be honored to be with a man like you. I've missed you. If I could go back, I'd do everything different."

"Differently," I say.

"Right, thanks," she says.

I can't believe she's doing this to me or that my body is reacting to her. "Are you done?" I ask.

"I guess so."

90

I rise from my desk. "I appreciate your thanks, and I accept your apology." That's all I have to say to Shante as I exit the room.

I'm halfway to my car when my little brother approaches. "What do you want, William?" I ask.

"I'm here to extend an olive branch," he says as he walks next to me.

"Why would you do that?"

"Father wants to bury the hatchet. No hard feelings. And he wants to meet with you."

"There's no hatchet to bury. I told you I don't want to see him."

"Why are you so angry?"

"You tell me. You grew up in that house just like I did. Why do you admire that man so much?"

"He's the only father I have."

I stop and push his shoulder. "You don't need him."

"Brother, our father insists on meeting with you. He told me to tell you he's not going to ask again."

"What could he possibly want with me?" I resume walking.

"He won't say. Maybe he wants to work with you."

"I would never work with that man, and he knows it."

"You know how he is. I can't go back and tell him I failed."

"That's the life you chose. Tell him I refused. Goodbye, brother."

William stops while I walk away. I wish things were different, but we've all made our choices.

IX ~ Shante

My attempt to make amends didn't quite go as planned. I think I expected him to take me in his arms and tell me he was waiting for me, but that's the kind of thing that happens in movies. I'm not going to let Jeremiah's attitude get to me. Today is a new day, and I'm getting him back, no matter what it takes.

I made good use of my time off. Jeremiah thought if I quit last semester, I'd never come back, but he was wrong. I'm back, and I'm prepared. I've studied him. I know as much about his career as I could find online.

He loves the law, and I figured if I showed him I was serious about class and the law, then he'd be impressed, but he didn't seem to care too much. Maybe he was pretending. He's way more stubborn than I am.

I get to school early, wearing a short, white skirt and a fitted pink shirt. I like the way this skirt flares. My hair is silky, my makeup is sultry, and I showered right before class. I wanted to smell fresh. Class is Monday and Wednesday, and I wanted to leave an impression on Jeremiah since I probably won't see him until next week.

"Look at you. Looking like a whole snack."

I turn around.

"It's good to see you again."

"Strike, right. How are you?" I say.

"Better now."

"Why is that?"

"The woman who stole my heart just reappeared. I didn't know if I would see you again," he says.

I blush, "As charming as I remember."

"What have you been up to?"

"I quit last semester, but I'm back."

"It's good to see you. Why don't we get that dinner we never had?"

"I don't know."

"Come on, Shante. You don't want to break my heart twice, do you?"

"Strike, I don't even know you."

"We can change that tonight. I'll tell you all about my hopes and dreams. Have dinner with me."

"I have to go. Can we talk later?"

"Give me your number."

I like his boldness, but I still have doubts about him. "Why don't you give me your number," I say.

I open my phone to add a new contact and hand it to him. "Put your real name in there," I say.

"I'll tell you over drinks," he says as he hands me my phone and walks away.

I look at the screen. He saved his name as Strike with a wink emoji.

I continue down the hall. I feel like it's the first day all over again. Jeremiah's office is difficult to find, but once I do, I step inside the room and close the door. "Hello, Jeremiah," I say.

"Hello," he says. His nostrils flare, and his eyes close, but he doesn't look up. He's writing something. I'm not moving from this spot until he looks at me.

"Jeremiah," I say to the top of his head.

"Yes, Miss Wilson?"

"I have a question for you."

He says nothing.

—

93

I'm agitated at this point. I tried to be classy, but he's being rude. "I thought you accepted my apology."

"That's not a question," he says.

"Here's a question for you. Why are you such a dick?"

He stands with anger in his eyes. "Shante," he yells, slamming his hands on his desk. Then he stops. He takes in my body, starting with my legs. His eyes change colors when they reach my breasts. I haven't seen them do that in a while.

"Your eyes," I say as I step around his desk, hypnotized. A flood of desire washes over me as his body faces mine. "What's your problem?" I yell.

"Lower your voice," he says.

"Tell me."

"I thought I'd never see you again. Why did you come back here?" he asks.

"Why does that bother you so much? You're such a jackass."

"Don't you say that to me?"

"Why not? It's true. I obviously came here for you, and to get an education or whatever, but you know I'm here for you. You're too busy being a dick to appreciate it. I apologized. I know I hurt you, but it was an awful moment for me. You have to understand. You said you wanted to be with me before. Did all that disappear?"

"What the fuck do you want from me, Shante? I've forgiven you, okay, but we need to move on. You can start. Drop my class."

"I'm not going anywhere. You're the one with the issue. You quit."

"Look at me. Pay attention to what I'm saying. I don't want you here, and I don't want you."

I raise my hand to slap him.

He grabs my wrist and holds it. "Don't put your hands on me," he says with a growl.

We stare at one another, our breaths labored, our bodies pressed together. He can't deny he wants me. I can feel exactly how much he wants me pressed against my stomach. "Why do you want me to leave? Is it too hard for you?" I ask.

"Don't be silly. I'm a professional."

"Are you sure? It's pretty hard from where I'm standing." I remove my arm from his grasp and place my arms around his neck. I stand on my tiptoes and inhale. I missed his scent.

He wraps his arms around my waist. The warmth of his body soothes me as I press myself as close as I can.

"Jeremiah, I missed you so much."

He growls.

"Hold me closer," I say.

He does. As he lays his head on my shoulder. The hairs on his beard prick my neck.

"Kiss me, my mate." I don't know what I'm saying. It reminds me of something I heard him say when we met. At the time, I thought it was romantic. It seems to affect him.

He's drawn to me. He lifts his head. Our lips meet, and when they press together, sparks fly. His mouth overpowers mine. I need this, need him. His hands roam my body and settle underneath my skirt. The feeling of his fingers against my skin electrifies me. I knew he still wanted me.

Our kiss becomes urgent. I'm eager to make up for lost time. I can't stop, and I never want to. He picks me up and sits me on the edge of his desk. He pulls my shirt and bra down, exposing my nipple. He immediately captures it with his teeth, pleasure courses through my veins. *We can skip the foreplay. I want to be fucked right now.*

I unbuckle his belt and unzip his pants. I've been waiting for this moment for three long months. I take him into my hand, hard, stiff, long, beautifully sculpted, and damnit it's going to be mine.

"I want you now," I say as I stroke his length.

I lay back on the desk and open my legs. I shriek when he rips my panties from my body. He caresses my legs and lifts them in the air, kissing his way down.

"Jeremiah," I call.

"Whose pussy is this?" he asks. He presses my clit and inserts his fingers, toying with my wetness. His eyes are fixated on me.

I moan. "Feels so good," I say.

"Whose pussy is this?" he asks again.

"It's yours, Jeremiah, all yours."

"We have to be quick," he says.

"Does this mean you forgive me?"

"I told you I do."

"Does this mean we can be together?" I ask.

"This means we each get what we want right now. I can't take my hands off you. We're together right now, and we should take advantage of this moment."

I'm a little disappointed. I know game when I hear it. This is not the Jeremiah I fell for. The first time we were in this position, he was sure he wanted to be with me right then. His behavior is different.

"I know you missed me, baby. Let me take care of you." His hands feel so good against my skin.

I thrust my hips, sinking his fingers inside me. The pleasure is excruciating, but my mind is reeling. I don't know what I want more, the pleasure of this moment, or the security of knowing I have his heart. The last time we made love, he pulled the rug from under me. I don't know if I could recover a second time around.

He presses his dick against my entrance and I close my eyes. He grabs my hair and holds my head up, guiding my body where he wants it. He wants me to see everything.

"Jeremiah," I say.

"Yes, baby."

"I need to know."

"Know what?"

"Do you want to be with me?"

"I can't answer that right now."

"Why not? You were sure before."

"Things are different now."

"But, before."

—

96

"Shante, my dear, your pussy is begging for me." He leans forward and kisses my neck.

My head rolls back. I do want to enjoy this moment.

He kisses my lips. "Jeremiah," I whisper.

"Say my name," he says.

"Jeremiah," I say.

"Tell me you want me."

"I want you so bad."

"Badly," he says.

"Really?"

He yanks my hair. "Don't talk back," he says.

"Sorry, Professor Johnson."

"Tell me you want this dick."

"I want this dick." I hold his head up until he looks into my eyes. "I want the man too. Can you tell me you want me, Jeremiah?"

He hesitates.

"Fuck." I shake my head.

"Shante, I—" He takes a deep breath. "I'm sorry."

"What?" I ask.

"This is a mistake," he says.

"A mistake? Why is this a mistake?"

He adjusts his clothes and zips his pants. "I apologize. I got carried away. Look, if you're going to remain in my class, we can't behave this way."

He adjusts my clothes and my hair as I hop off the desk.

"Why did you do this to me?"

"You should leave."

"That's how it is? This is how you're going to treat me?"

He sits at his desk. "Why don't you head to class? I'll see you there."

"Fuck that," I say. "We need to talk."

"No, we don't, Shante. We've talked. We're done talking. I don't want to talk anymore. I can't deal with you."

"You can't deal with me? That's hilarious."

—

97

"Jeremiah," a woman's voice sings his name as she approaches the door.

He clears his throat.

A young woman opens the door and peeks her head into the room. She's pretty. "Oh, sorry, Professor Johnson. I didn't know you had a visitor. I'll see you tonight," she says as she waves and walks away.

"Who was that?" I snap.

"None of your business," he says.

"Are you sleeping with her?"

"I don't answer to you, Shante."

"Like hell, you don't. Let me find out you're messing with some bitch."

"I'm not going to tell you again what I do is none of your concern." He looks at his watch. "I have to get to class. If I were you, I wouldn't be late. Now, if you'll excuse me." He grabs his things and heads for the door.

"Why are you acting like a bitch?"

He turns around, his anger evident. I take a step backward. Damn, he's sexy in his sweater vest when he's angry. "Shante, keep fucking with me, and we're going to have a problem."

"Are you going to teach me a lesson, professor? Are you going to put me over your knee and spank me? I think I'd like that."

"Bend over," he says.

"Excuse me?"

"Bend over," he commands.

I roll my eyes.

"Just like I thought. All talk," he says.

"Oh, really?" I bend over and remember he has my panties. My bare ass is in the air.

He pops me on my behind. I jump. His hand is firm, and I feel a sting. "Hands behind your back," he says.

I bring my hands together, and he holds them in place in the middle of my back.

"Have you learned your lesson?"

"Are you done acting like a bitch?"

98

"Lift that ass," he says.

I stand on my tiptoes.

He growls and gives me another pop.

The sting feels so good.

He holds his hand in place. "Have you learned your lesson?"

"Harder."

Another pop.

I growl.

He bites my ear and whispers, "I know you want more, don't you?"

"Mmmm," I moan.

"I know you want more, but Big Daddy has a class to teach."

I straighten up as he opens the door and walks out of the room.

Jeremiah may be angry with me. He may even be hesitant about us, but I know one thing, when he's with me, his rules and his professional behavior go out the window. He can barely control himself.

I smile. I still got him. I just have to wear him down. But first, I need to go to the bathroom and wipe myself off. I'm dripping wet, and I have no underwear. I can't sit in my chair like this.

I walk into the classroom one minute before six o'clock with a sigh of relief.

"Glad you could make it, Miss Wilson."

"I wouldn't dream of missing your class, Professor Johnson." I take my seat, carefully making sure my skirt covers my bottom. His eyes avoid looking at me. Damn, I wanted to wink at him or something. He's denying me this moment.

I see a familiar face walk by the classroom. He sees me too.

"Hey, Shante," he shouts as he stops in the doorway.

My eyes widen in horror.

"Shante, you can't hear me speaking to you?"

Everyone laughs.

"Professor, can you do something about this?" Amber asks. I knew she was a hater.

Jeremiah is visibly upset. There's a vein popping out of his forehead.

"Shante, you're breaking my heart. Can I at least get a hi?" he yells. I knew Strike was trouble.

"Hi," I say as I wave him off.

Strike puts his hand over his heart and smiles back at me.

Jeremiah rushes to the door. He and Strike back up into the hallway, and I can't hear anything. I look and strain my ears, but I get nothing.

Jeremiah walks back into the room like a raging bull. He points at me. "Shante, please tell your boyfriends to refrain from disturbing my class."

"I can't control what he does," I say.

"The rest of us would appreciate it," Amber says.

"I'll keep that in mind, Amber, wouldn't want to make anyone jealous," I say in the fakest voice I can muster.

There are faint snickers throughout the room.

"Let's settle down and begin." Jeremiah acts as if nothing happens and jumps right into today's class.

I make it my mission to show off once again by answering all the questions before Amber can. It's obvious she has a thing for Jeremiah. I know she's fuming. *Better find another man, bitch. This one's taken.*

When class is over, I pretend I'm writing something in my notebook as everyone leaves. It's me, Jeremiah, and Amber left in the room. I know she's trying to wait me out, but I've got nothing but time.

"Shante, is it?" she asks.

"You know what it is," I say without looking at her.

"Could you give me a moment with Professor Johnson? I need to discuss something privately with him."

"OMG, Amber, I didn't realize. I absolutely cannot. If you need to say something to the professor, it should be something everyone could hear. We wouldn't want there to be some sort of incident. These things could get tricky.

You know, the *he said, she said*. So, you go right ahead and say what you need to say." I sit with my chin in my hand and continue to write in my notebook.

"I can wait. Why don't you go ahead?" Amber says.

I bet Jeremiah's loving this. "I'm writing something down before I forget. You won't even know I'm here," I say.

"You know what, I'll talk to you later, Professor Johnson."

"Goodnight, Amber," he says.

Once she leaves the room, I burst out laughing.

"You're ridiculous," Jeremiah says to me.

"I can't help myself. Someone has a crush on the teacher. You'd better do something about her before I do."

"You're acting territorial."

"It's not an act," I say.

"Shante." He can't hide his smirk this time. "I have to go." He gathers his things.

"Can I have a goodnight kiss, Jeremiah?"

"Why don't you ask your boyfriend?"

"He's not my boyfriend."

"Your personal life is none of my business."

"It could be."

"Can I give you some advice?"

"What's that?"

"Stay away from Strike." He grits his teeth, barely saying his name. "He's not the kind of guy you should be involved with."

"Do you know him?"

"Listen to me for once. Stay away from him."

"You're not jealous, are you?"

"No."

"Glad to hear it. So I can be friends with whoever I choose."

"You do whatever you want." He walks away.

I finally gather my things and leave the classroom, feeling empty. Once I don't have Jeremiah there to taunt, everything I've done seems stupid. I've never had to work this hard to get a man's attention, but I was the one who fucked up, so I figure I have to fix it. What would Nana do? I told her what happened with Brian, and she told me to be patient with Jeremiah because he's a proud man. She said I needed to learn how to deal with an alpha, and I've never had to before. I never got to ask her what she meant by that. She and I agreed I blew it, but by the time I realized it, I had already left school.

I cut my losses, and then he caught me when I was falling. There's something about Jeremiah I can't let go of. Moving on is impossible. He's imprinted in my brain, my body. I crave him in an indescribable way. I don't know what to do with these feelings, and it's driving me crazy.

As I walk through the hallways to my car, I see the young woman from earlier. I replay the way she sang his name when she walked by his office. She said she would see him tonight. Please tell me Jeremiah isn't fucking this girl with the long legs and pretty face.

"Shante."

I turn around.

"Shante, slow down."

"Hi, Strike. You like embarrassing me, don't you?"

"I like to make you smile," Strike says.

"I'm kind of in a hurry," I say. I look ahead to make sure I still have eyes on the girl.

"How's now."

"For what?"

"Our date. I'm here, and you're here."

"Tonight's not good. Sorry, handsome." We walk out the door.

"Tell me when."

"I don't know. I have a lot going on."

"So do I," he says.

"I'll call you. I have to go. See you later."

He grabs my hand and looks into my eyes. His eyes change colors, a bright blue. "Don't make me wait."

I blush. "I have to go." I turn around, and he slowly releases my hand.

The girl gets into her car. It's not far from mine. I have to follow her and find out what's going on for myself. Dating Brian taught me how to follow someone without getting caught. This won't be a problem. I guess that was the takeaway from that pointless relationship. I hang back as I trail behind her car. It's dark, and I don't recognize where we're going. There are no restaurants or bars this way. No houses. We're moving away from civilization.

She slows down and puts on her turn signal. *Where is she going?* There's nothing here but woods. Why is she stopping here alone? Is this where she's meeting Jeremiah?

I slow down as she parks her car outside the woods and gets out. There are other cars there. I pass her up, so she doesn't know she's being followed.

Shouldn't I keep going and take my ass home? Do I want to risk my life for this shit? I'm already here. There's no way I'm going home without knowing. I won't be able to sleep. There's no reason for a young woman to be out here, and definitely not with Jeremiah.

I turn around and pull in where the other cars are parked. No one is standing by the cars, so I can sneak in and out. I see smoke in the distance. They must have lit a fire. Is this supposed to be romantic? Is it an orgy?

I grab my cellphone. It's so dark out here. I must be crazy. "Think about what you're doing, Shante. No man is worth this," I say to myself. Maybe no man is worth this, but Jeremiah is. I take a deep breath as I open the car door and step into the night.

Looking around, I only see bushes and trees. Did she just walk into the forest? Before I move, I open my Maps. It says I'm in Blue Ridge Forest. I turn on my phone's flashlight and look around behind the cars. There's a path. This must be where everyone headed.

This is by far the stupidest thing I've ever done. I walk to the path with my phone in front of me. This is my last chance to turn around. The flashlight allows me to see well enough. If things get weird, I can always turn around. I walk through the trees and the bushes. I hope there are no animals out here. I didn't even think about that.

I tell myself to breathe. My stomach turns flips when I'm pretty deep in the forest. The trail is no longer a trail at this point. I'm following the smoke. How am I going to get out of here? Why didn't I drop a pin? I look at my Maps. I'm relieved it shows where my car is parked.

I've never been this deep in the woods before. I'm close to where the fire is. I think I hear voices. I look at my phone. Now I have no signal. *Shit*. At least I'm not out here alone.

Once I see the flames I cut off my flashlight and tiptoe to a tree. There's a group, maybe thirty people sitting at picnic tables around the fire. Someone says something, and they all howl. What is this? There's barbecue and drinks. Are they having a party?

My heart skips a beat when I spot Jeremiah. He stands to applause and cheers. I think I hear barking. He's wearing a t-shirt and jeans, and he looks good. All eyes are on him. He uses his hands to settle the crowd. He howls, and everyone howls back. He shouts something I can't make out, but whatever it is, it gets everyone riled up. They all start chanting. "Blue Ridge, Blue Ridge."

"What?" I say to myself. Maybe they're a secret society. It looks like Jeremiah is in charge. I jump when music starts blasting.

Is that rap? Jeremiah listens to this? Everyone starts dancing and drinking. Jeremiah stands back and rocks to the beat. He's going through the motions. He doesn't seem happy. The woman I followed dances in front of him.

He smiles at her as she gets a little too close for my liking. I don't know what the hell he's smiling at. She holds out her hand and invites him to dance, beckoning him with her index finger. He politely declines, and she walks off.

I smile to myself. "Damn right."

"What are you doing here?" A man's voice whispers in my ear.

I gasp.

Someone grabs the back of my neck. I scream. "Let go of me." I try to push him off me, but he's way too strong.

Everything goes quiet, and I hear Jeremiah's voice. "Bring her to me."

X ~ Jeremiah

I swear Shante has made it her mission in life to torment me.

Jonathan walks an agitated Shante to me. "Alpha, I found her spying on us."

"Is that true?" I ask Shante.

"I'm not spying on anyone. Get your hand off me before I break it."

Jonathan laughs. "She's funny. Can we keep her?" he asks.

"This one is trouble," I say.

"She's harmless, and if she acts up, I can think of a few ways to keep her in line," Jonathan says.

My wolf makes his displeasure known.

He looks at Shante, then at me. His eyes widen. "I'm sorry, Alpha. I didn't know."

I look at Shante. "What the hell are you doing here?"

She struggles to break free of Jonathan's grip on her arm.

"Let her go. I'll deal with her."

"Yes, Alpha," he says before he turns away.

"Turn the music back on," I shout. I turn to Shante. "Explain yourself."

"I don't have to explain anything," she says.

"You need to tell me why you're here and how you found me. You didn't follow me here, so tell me, or I'm going to believe you're a spy. You don't want to know what we do to spies."

"It's a free country. I can go wherever I want."

"Shante, my patience is running out. You're taking this game of yours too far. You're going to have to move on with your life. You could've put yourself in danger."

"Would you hurt me?" she asks.

"I'd never hurt you, but everyone isn't like me."

"Maybe you wouldn't hurt me physically."

"What are you talking about?"

"Forget it. You're so arrogant. Everything is not about you?"

"Why else would you be here?"

"I was taking a walk."

"Out here? In the dark?"

"Yes, I come here all the time."

"I've never seen you here once. As a matter of fact, you're trespassing."

"I guess we just always miss one another," she shrugs.

"Go home," I say.

"What are you doing out here?" she asks.

"None of your business, and don't pull this again. You have no idea what you're doing."

"Why do you try so hard to push me away? You can't be this cold."

"What if I am? Would that make you leave me alone?"

"You're not."

"Why do you insist on torturing me?"

"How am I torturing you? By breathing?"

"Leave it alone."

"You mean, leave you alone. I don't understand why you're still mad at me."

"I'm not mad."

"Why do you act like you can't be in the same room with me? You want me. Don't try to deny it."

"You should go."

A group starts dancing our way, drunk and shouting. "Alpha, what are you doing? It's your birthday. You should be dancing with the pretty girl."

There are whispers among my pack about why I'm giving Shante a hard time and how it's obvious she's my mate. Shifters know the body never lies. Her heartbeat matches my own, and the pheromones are undeniable. "Give us a minute?" I say.

They dance away, and I pull Shante away from the crowd.

"It's your birthday?" she asks.

"Yes."

"You know what I wished for all these months?" she asks.

"What?" I ask.

"That I could spend nights like this with you."

"You're killing me."

"I'm telling the truth."

"Why now, Shante? Why did you come back?" I ask.

"I had to process things here." She grabs my hand and places it at her temple. "And here," she places my hand over her heart.

"What do you want from me? I was ready to give you this." I place her hand over my heart. I wonder if she can feel my heartbeat. "You told me you could never be with someone like me, and you had a long list of reasons."

"I've apologized."

"I appreciate your apology, but now I want to move on." I drop her hand.

"I didn't mean it. You know that."

"I told you I forgave you."

"So you keep saying, but it's not true."

"I don't know what I can do to show you I'm sincere."

"Why don't I stay for the party?"

"I don't think that's a good idea."

"Come on. You know you want me here," she says.

"That might not be a good idea. I don't want to confuse you, Shante."

"I'm a big girl. I can handle anything you've got."

"I don't like making you feel bad, but I don't want to give you any false hope."

Sadness creeps across her face, but she quickly recovers.

I feel like shit because I know she has feelings for me. Every time I reject her, it kills me.

She changes the subject. "I can't believe you're partying on a school night. Don't you have work tomorrow?"

"I'm a night owl."

"I assumed you'd be in bed by nine and up at the crack of dawn."

"You haven't learned yet."

"Learned what?"

"I'm more than you think I am. You think you want to be with me, but I'm more than an arrogant, judgmental, asshole you could never love."

"I know you're more than that, Jeremiah. I didn't mention that you were the kind, generous, thoughtful man who excites me and surprises me, and makes my heart race when you look into my eyes. You're the man who wouldn't let me quit when I was determined to give up. You're the man who bought a battery for my car and told me it was free because you knew I was too proud to accept help. The man who got that car washed and cleaned for me."

My heart leaps in my chest. "Shante, stop."

"You're the man who kept his promise to my Nana, and visited her while she was dying, and who picked me up when I couldn't stand."

I clear my throat.

"I know exactly who you are. Do you know who I am?"

"You're the woman who inspired me to do those things," I say.

109

"Is it so hard for you to love me?"

"No, Shante. It's easy. That's the problem."

"Are you sorry you met me?"

"Of course not."

"I can work with that."

"That's not an invitation to keep trying."

"Why do all these people call you Alpha? What is this?"

That's not a conversation I'm about to have with her nosey ass. I grab her hand and lead her back to the party. She smiles when my pack cheers as we join them.

I wind my hips to the flow of the reggae song, and she turns around, pressing her body into mine. With her hand holding the back of my head, we fit together like puzzle pieces as we grind against one another. The songs change, the tempo is faster. She smiles at me as we dance. I'm happy to see the joy on her face and the way her eyes light up when she looks at me. A twinge of regret pinches my heart.

The music slows down, and I pull her body close. Her skin glistens from the sweat. I inhale her scent. "I love the smell of your skin," I say.

She lays her head on my chest as we move side to side. "I'm glad I came."

"It's not the worst thing in the world, I guess," I say.

"Jeremiah, you're such a sweet talker."

"That's what the ladies tell me."

"Really, what ladies?"

"Don't ruin the moment."

"I will find out."

I hold up her chin. "Hey."

"What?"

"Would you like something to drink?"

"Sure."

I walk her to one of the tables. "I'll be right back."

"Okay."

I take a deep breath. I can't think straight when she's around. I still don't know what the hell she's doing here or

110

how she found me, but I have to admit to myself it is nice to have her here, amongst my pack on my birthday.

"Thank you," she says as I hand her a beer. She takes a drink, and a bit pours down the corner of her lip.

I wipe it away with my thumb.

"I must look like a mess," she says.

"You look beautiful." I tuck her hair behind her ear and hold her cheek in my palm.

"You're being nice."

"You always look beautiful."

"Jeremiah," she gushes. Those simple words from me make her smile.

She places her hand over mine. "Kiss me," she says.

"I'm trying not to complicate things," I say.

"It's too late. They're already complicated." She's right. "Can I just give you a birthday kiss?"

I lean in. My face is an inch from hers. If I kiss her, I may not be able to stop. I try to focus on the music blasting. My wolf has visions of the look on her face when I claim her, of her having my pups, and desire takes over my mind and body.

Her lips crash into mine, and our beers crash to the floor. I'm reminded of everything I let go. I pushed her away months ago. Maybe I was a fool. The hunger I feel for her unleashes. I need to feel her body, the warmth of her skin. I place my hands underneath her skirt and squeeze her fat ass.

She moans into my mouth. She's as desperate for me as I am for her. I groan when she grabs my hand and positions it between her legs. Moisture coats my fingers, and I'm captivated by the scent of her essence as I explore her pussy. She lifts her leg against my body as we move to the rhythm of the music. Her hands wrap around my neck, and my thumb massages her clit. She whispers my name in my ear. I can't contain my growl, and I can't contain my want.

I lift Shante over my shoulder and carry her away.

"Where are we going?" she asks.

"To fuck."

"Whatever Big Daddy wants."

"Big Daddy wants you." Without thinking, I hold on to Shante and take off running.

Shante screams my name. "How can you run so fast?" she yells.

I don't reply.

She holds her arms out.

I take her to a spot I think she'll love and stand her up. The music from the party can still be heard in the distance.

"Don't do me like you did last time."

I look in her eyes. "I won't." I spare her the pretense that I don't know what she's talking about.

She sways her hips and teases me with the look in her eyes. "The tulips are beautiful," she says.

"Take your clothes off."

"Yes, professor."

"Call me, Alpha."

"Yes, Alpha." She removes her clothes piece by piece as she dances for me.

I remove my shirt.

"Take off your pants," she says.

"No."

She looks startled.

"You don't tell me what to do. Understand?"

"Yes, Alpha."

"Come here," I say.

She walks to me. "What would you have me do?" she asks.

I say nothing.

She grabs my belt.

"Ask," I say.

She unbuckles it.

"Can I take off your pants, Alpha?"

"It's may I," I say.

"May I get fucked without you correcting my English, Alpha?"

"You will take everything I give you."

I roll my eyes.

"You will not roll your eyes at me or disrespect me again, and the correct response is, yes, Alpha."

"Can we stop talking?" she asks as she unbuckles my belt and unzips my pants.

"On your knees."

She obeys.

I step out of my pants and shoes and stand directly in front of her. "Keep your eyes on my dick. You are going to take every inch into your mouth. Do you understand?" I remove my shirt.

She nods.

"What did I tell you?"

"Yes, Alpha." Her eyes follow my dick as it moves up and down.

"Can you handle that?"

She bites her lip. I enjoy her excitement. "May I begin, Alpha?"

"You may."

"Thank you," she says.

I grab her hair and give her head a firm yank backward. "You will not disappoint me. Do you understand?"

"Yes, Alpha."

She opens her mouth and takes me in her hand. My body tingles when she sucks the tip and takes all of my dick, holds it in her mouth.

"Good job," I say. I feel the tension leaving my body.

"Thank you, Alpha."

"Did I tell you to stop?"

She takes me in her mouth again. There's passion in every movement, every slurp. She massages my balls with one hand and my dick with the other.

"That's right. Suck your Alpha's dick."

I grab the back of her head and thrust into her mouth. This shit feels so good. I can tell she's made for me. She's capable of taking all of me. That's not an easy feat. She gives me pleasure I've never known. With a growl, I remove myself from the grasp of her mouth and lay her down on the bed of tulips. They crush underneath our weight. "Open your mouth."

Shante is compliant like I've never seen her before. I prop myself on my hands and stick my dick in her mouth. Once again, she's eager to please. Her mouth is warm and wet, and ecstasy courses through my body. She takes my entire dick into her mouth as I push myself in and out, again and again.

"Fuck, Shante. You feel so fucking good."

She moans as her mouth meets my thrusts.

I circle my hips and hold still. "You will swallow," I command.

I feel my release coming as my pumps grow more furious. I can't slow down. I give all I've got, and she takes it. My dick continuously hits the back of her throat. I should bow to her. I growl, and I don't hold back as I release. She sucks harder as my seed pours into her mouth. My body convulses, my toes curl, and my mind goes blank. She swallows every drop, and all I can think is happy birthday to me.

"Did you like that, Alpha?"

"I'm very pleased. You did well." As I exhale, I move my naked body to cover hers. I brush a lock of hair from her face. "Tell your Alpha what you want."

"I want you to fuck me like an animal."

"Like an animal? What kind of animal? A kitten?"

"No, like a beast."

"I know what you want. You want me to fuck you like a wolf?"

"Yes, like a wolf. Fuck me like a wolf."

My dick is instantly hard. I can't contain my growl. My canines descend, and I fight to hold back. My claws attempt to come out. The wolf wants to break free.

"Are you okay?" she asks.

I take a moment to compose myself. "I'm okay." I pry her legs open with my knee. The aroma of her desire overpowers my thinking. Without warning, I enter her with a single thrust. She cries out, screaming my name as I fuck her tight pussy with a wild fury she's never experienced before. I don't even think I've experienced it before. My body craves hers, and I push myself into her depths. I lift her leg over my shoulder and drive into her from an angle.

Her nails dig into my back, and it only makes me go harder. Our lips crash together in a messy kiss. I bite her lip until I taste blood. She moans. She has no idea what she asked for, and as much as I love it, she loves it more. Out here in nature, my home, my territory, I want to mate her. I want to claim her. I can't stop myself from marking her. I dig my claws into her upper thigh and scratch. My body tingles, and hers convulses.

Her pussy grips me. She's about to come. I want to bite her neck, but I hesitate. "Jeremiah," she cries. I capture her mouth as she comes.

As she tries to catch her breath, I flip her over. "On your knees," I say. She wanted a beast, and she got one.

I enter her from behind as I hold on to her hips. She screams. This is not a scream of ecstasy. It takes a second to register. It's fear.

XI ~ Shante

Jeremiah takes my breast into his hand. My head rolls back, and I open my eyes.

Angry, green eyes flicker in front of my face. I scream. This man is older. He looks like Jeremiah, dark brown skin, tall, muscular, and that same chiseled jaw.

"Please don't stop on our account. You're quite talented, Shante. I'm impressed."

I scream again. I'm frantic. Jeremiah pulls out and we jump to our feet. I try to remember where my clothes are, but they're a few feet away. "What the fuck is going on? I don't know what's going on. Jeremiah, what's going on?"

"Now, I see why you were in a hurry today," Strike says to me.

Jeremiah picks his shirt up off the ground. "Put this on."

I put on the shirt and hold on to Jeremiah, who's still naked.

Jeremiah grabs my hand. "I won't let anything happen to you."

"Stand down," Jeremiah shouts.

Who is he talking to? I look around, and all I see are eyes, pairs of eyes in various shades, staring at us. I squirm and dig my nails into Jeremiah's arm. He grabs me and kisses my forehead.

"It's okay. You're safe," he says. "My pack will protect you."

I'm not sure what that means, but I trust him. I find comfort in his embrace. My eyes focus, and I can make out one of the figures. It's a wolf. I blink. They're all wolves.

"Jeremiah?" I question him.

He nods, and I know what I'm seeing is real. I'm surrounded by a pack of wolves. My Nana used to put me to bed with stories about wolves. She said we shouldn't be afraid of wolves because they're our friends, here to help us. I thought that was something she made up. That she was obsessed with the animal. She has paintings and figurines of wolves. I thought she was crazy. I guess she knew something I didn't, and I can only assume Jeremiah is one of them. Although he can't just be one of them. They respect him. He's their alpha.

"Strike, what are you doing here?" I shout.

"My big brother has been ignoring me." He points to Jeremiah.

"Your brother?" I ask Jeremiah.

"Half-brother," Jeremiah says.

"He's your brother," the old man says.

"You turned me down for him?" Strike asks.

"You idiot. We're not here so you can flirt with this slut," the old man says to Strike.

Strike tries to hide his shame, but his head falls briefly before he picks it up. I see it in his eyes. Nothing he does is good enough for his father. It's the same thing Jeremiah struggles with.

"Bite your tongue, or I'll tear it out. Don't you ever say that about her," Jeremiah says.

"Your brother told me you've refused to see me. Did you think I would just let that go. I was kind enough to extend an invitation. Don't forget I'm your father," the green-eyed older man says.

"James, let me be clear. You are nothing to me," Jeremiah says to his father.

"You show me the fucking respect I deserve," James says.

"Get out of my forest, James. You don't deserve my respect."

"You can be mad at me, son, if that makes you feel better about yourself, but don't you ever think you're a self-made man," James says.

"You're a piece of work. I haven't heard from you since I left your home, and now you want to take credit for my success," Jeremiah says.

"Damn right. You are my son. I did raise you. I taught you how to be a man, and you carried me with you wherever you went. You got a career, started a pack, and became a man because of me. Tell me you don't think about me every time you negotiate a deal, or when you make a decision about your little pack."

"My pack is greater than yours will ever be," Jeremiah says. "Do you know why? I know how to treat people. I know how to value them. My pack is strong, in the jungle, and in the real world."

"You ungrateful fool. You will respect me. I made you." He stands eye to eye with Jeremiah. "I'm your alpha, and you'd better not forget it."

"You bullied me, belittled me, and beat me. You were a pathetic excuse for a man who took his frustrations out on a child who couldn't defend himself."

"And look who you became. I had to be hard on you because life is hard. No one's going to hold your fucking hand and walk you through it. You should be on your knees, thanking me for molding you. You look like me, you walk like me, you talk like me, and no matter how hard you try you'll never be rid of me. You are me."

"Should I thank you for trying to kill me? Should I thank you for that? I almost died at the claws of my so-called father. Who does that?"

118

"But you didn't. You picked yourself up, and you made something of your life. I know how to kill. If I wanted you dead, you'd be dead. You're welcome, son."

"Fuck you. You sadistic bastard," Jeremiah yells.

"Don't talk to him like that," Strike says.

James points to Strike. "You shut up and learn something. You waste your time running the streets like a common thug."

"I don't run the streets. I own the streets," Strike says.

"You own nothing. You do what I allow you to do. The streets are mine," James says.

"I don't care what you two do. Get out of my territory," Jeremiah says.

"I came all the way here to talk to you. The least you can do is listen," James says.

Strike rolls his eyes. "What do you want with him that's so important?"

I rub Jeremiah's back. He's tense and furious. "You don't have to do this," I say.

"Shut up, and stay in your place. You're not worthy of being in my presence or my son's," James says.

Jeremiah's fists ball, but I grab his hand and nod. "It's okay, Jeremiah." I turn to his father. "You are a disrespectful bastard, and Jeremiah is nothing like you. He's more of a man, and more of an alpha than you will ever be, you pathetic, old, son of a bitch. Don't try to take credit for what he's achieved. You should be bowing to him. Looks like he taught you more than you ever taught him, and I don't need anyone to fight for me. You say one more thing about Shante, and I'll rip your tongue out my damn self."

Jeremiah and Strike are stunned.

James scoffs. "I don't have time for this. The time has come for you to take your rightful place as alpha of the family pack."

"I already have a pack," Jeremiah says.

"Him," Strike shouts. "You want him to take over. That's what you had to talk about."

"Did I stutter?" James says.

Strike paces and throws his hands in the air. He turns red. "I can't believe you would do this to me. I've been by your side this whole time. He ran away."

"You're not ready," James says.

"Not ready? I've been running shit. Your pack respects me a hell of a lot more than they respect you. You old fool."

James slaps Strike. "Watch your fucking mouth."

Jeremiah moves my body behind his.

Strike laughs as he wipes blood from his lip. He steps to his father with his finger pointed in the man's face. "That's the last time you will ever touch me."

"You will respect me," James shouts.

"I'd appreciate it if you two would take your family issues elsewhere. I don't want your pack. William can have it. Goodnight."

"Is she the reason?" James asks. He runs toward us in the blink of an eye and grabs me by the neck.

I try to scream, but I can barely breathe as his grip sinks into my skin. He takes off running. I attempt to break free of his grasp, but he's too strong. That doesn't stop me from attempting to pry his fingers off me. Without warning, he releases me, and I fall to the ground. I grab my throat, coughing in an attempt to catch my breath. When I look up, Jeremiah has his father pinned on the ground, punching him in the face. All of a sudden, Jeremiah's body changes. I wouldn't believe it if I hadn't seen it with my own eyes.

He transforms into a wolf, a magnificent creature with a shiny grey coat and golden-brown eyes. Those eyes stare at me before he turns to his father and claws into him. His father transforms. They're huge, but Jeremiah still has his father pinned, and he's relentless. The eyes that were in the distance close in on us, but no one jumps in. Instead, they howl. Then Jeremiah howls.

"Stop," I yell.

A hand grabs my shoulder. I jump.

"Are you okay?" Strike asks.

Tears fall from my face, and Strike holds me in his arms.

"I'm sorry this happened. It's okay," he comforts me. "I wouldn't let my father hurt you," Strike says.

I nod.

"Why do you want my brother and not me?" Strike asks.

"Now isn't the time. You need to stop him before he kills your father," I say.

"Why would I do that? I can let him take care of the problem. You see how terrible my father is."

"Stop him now, or you'll both regret it."

Strike stands there with his arms folded.

"Jeremiah, stop," I scream. I'm too scared to get close to them.

Jeremiah growls.

"Strike," I yell. "Do something."

He's stubborn too.

"Please," I beg. "Stop him."

Strike grabs my hands, and his eyes turn blue. "The only reason I'm going to stop him from killing that bastard is because of you. My brother is not the one for you. I care about you, Shante. I mean it."

What the fuck? I thought Strike was just a flirt. I hope he's playing around.

Strike shifts into a blue eyed, grey wolf and charges into Jeremiah, knocking him off his dad. His father lies on the ground, whimpering, barely moving. I actually feel sorry for the old bastard.

Jeremiah growls as he jumps. He spins mid-air, landing on Strike's back.

"Damn," I yell. I didn't think a big ass wolf could jump like that.

Strike struggles to shake Jeremiah off, but Jeremiah sinks his nails into Strike. They howl and bark. It seems like they're communicating.

"Jeremiah, stop it. That's your brother," I yell. He's not paying attention to me. I need to do something. I walk toward the two wolves. James still lays on the ground, badly beaten.

I wait for an opening and tap Jeremiah on his back. His head whips around. "Please stop," I beg.

His eyes light up. He jumps off his brother's back and stalks closer to me. "I need you. Come to me," I say. His focus is on me, and he obeys. I hold out my hand and rub his fur. It's so soft and little sweaty. I can feel his heartbeat. I wrap my arms around his neck and hold tight. "I'm okay, Jeremiah." He nuzzles against me. He calms down, and before I know it, Jeremiah is in front of me again.

He stands and turns to Strike, who is standing over his father. "Get him out of here. I don't want to see either of you again."

Strike looks at me, and I nod.

"I'm only doing this for you," he says to me.

"Thank you," I say.

Jeremiah's nostrils flare, and I rub his back.

The pack howls at Jeremiah. He howls back at them. "Everything's fine," he says. "Let's call it a night."

Strike tosses his father over his shoulder without any consideration for his injuries and takes off running.

I don't know what to say to Jeremiah. "Are you okay?" I ask.

"Fine," he says.

I hesitate. "Thank you for saving me."

"Don't mention it."

"I know this must've been hard for you."

"It's okay."

"Do you want to talk about it?"

"I'm fine." He walks faster.

I know he must be tired of my questions, but I don't know what to do. "Are you sure?" I ask.

"I'm fine, Shante. Stop asking me. I'm fine."

We walk through the forest and find our clothes.

"Let's get out of here." I put on my skirt as he puts on his pants. I quietly follow him back to the party area.

XII ~ Jeremiah

I walk Shante to my car and hold the door open. "Get in," I say.

"My car is right there," she points.

"I'll have someone take care of your car. You're staying with me tonight." I'd grabbed her keys and phone when we were on our way out. I throw her keys to my beta, Jonathan, and he assures me, through our mind link, that he'd take care of it. I hand Shante her phone.

"If you say so," she says.

I feel her excitement, but I don't want to talk to her. Anger courses through my veins.

"Are we going to your house?" she asks.

"No, I don't know if that's safe for you."

"I'm safe wherever I'm with you," she says.

I'm trying to fight the anger. I don't want to lash out at her.

"Do you want to talk about it?" she asks.

"I told you to stop with the questions."

"It's just that you've been through a lot tonight."

"I've been through a lot tonight because of you. You weren't even supposed to be here. Now, I have to worry about protecting you on top of everything I'm already dealing with."

"You don't have to worry about me. I can take care of myself," I snap.

"How were you going to take care of yourself if my father," I catch myself, "that man slit your throat? You don't listen."

"Maybe you should've let him do it. That would be one less thing for you to have to worry about."

"Don't you say that shit to me, Shante. You know I wouldn't let him hurt you."

"I don't know what to think anymore. You don't have to burden yourself with looking out for me, Jeremiah. I don't need you holding anything else over my head."

I'm seething, and I have nothing to say to her at the moment.

She pulls out her cellphone and starts browsing through it.

"How the fuck do you know William?" I ask.

"Who?" she shouts.

"William. Strike. How do you know my brother?"

"I don't really know him at all."

"He seems to be awfully smitten for someone who doesn't know you."

"What am I supposed to say to that?"

"Nothing."

"Are you jealous?"

"Hell no. I told you to stay away from him, and now you see why."

"He only wants your father's approval. You can understand that. He stopped you from killing your father tonight."

"Because you asked him to."

"I was trying to help you."

"I don't need your help."

"Well, he did it, and I'm glad he did. He tried to do something nice. Maybe you should cut him some slack."

"You don't know what you're talking about, and you don't know what kind of man he is. Just because you bat your eyelashes and he jumped to obey doesn't mean there's anything good about him."

"Why are we arguing about him? I don't want your brother."

I don't say anything.

She touches my arm. "I'm serious."

"Fine."

"Jeremiah, I don't even know him. He flirted with me a couple of times. That's it. I don't have any involvement with him."

"Yeah, okay."

"You believe me, don't you?"

"Yeah."

"In case I haven't made myself clear over the last couple of days, I want you and only you." She takes my free hand and intertwines her fingers with mine.

I'm upset that my body will always react to her touch.

She kisses my hand. "You told me about your father, but you never told me it was that bad," she says.

"Yep," I reply.

"If you want to talk about it, I'm here," she says.

"Thanks."

The rest of the ride is quiet.

"This is where you're staying." We arrive at a smaller property I own.

I bought the place under a shell corporation, so no one knows it belongs to me. My beta lives next door, so I know Shante will be safe here.

"Do I even have a say in the matter?" she asks.

"No, you don't."

She rolls her eyes as I hold her door open and extend my hand. "Is this your house, too?" she asks.

"Yes."

"Must be nice," she says.

I grab the keys out of the glove compartment and escort her inside. "Make yourself at home," I say.

"I'd like to take a shower and go to bed," she says.

"You've had a long night. I'm going to go, and I'll see you in the morning."

"Jeremiah," she grabs my arm and clenches, "no."

"You're safe. I promise."

"Please," she begs. She's trembling. I didn't take into consideration the trauma she must've experienced. I was so busy being angry.

"Okay. I'll stay."

"Thank you." She holds on tight.

"You don't have to thank me. I wasn't thinking," I say. I wrap my arms around her and kiss the top of her head.

I show her around the house. "This is nice," she says. "Do you have it on standby for damsels in distress?"

I laugh. "I can't deal with any damsels. You already give me enough of a headache. This is an investment."

"I've got something you can invest in," she says.

"What's that?"

"A shower. You stink."

"You know you love it," I say.

"Maybe I do," she says.

"Why don't you go ahead and do what you need to do? Everything you need is in the bathroom?"

"Yes, Alpha," she says as she saunters off.

Damnit. My dick goes hard as I watch her hips sway.

I hear the shower turn on, and I take a deep breath as I walk to the kitchen and grab a beer. I take a long sip and exhale. I have to strategize. I need to figure out how bad this is going to get.

I pick up the phone and call Jonathan.

"Hello," he picks up on the first ring.

"How's everything?"

"Fine. I'm on the way with the car now."

"Good. Shante's going to stay here for a while. I need you to keep an eye on her. Give her space. She doesn't need to know."

"Okay."

127

"If anything happens to her, I will kill you."

"Yes, Alpha. I understand."

"Good."

"Jeremiah," Shante calls from the bathroom.

"I have to go." I hang up and run to the door. "Is everything okay?"

"I need help," she says.

"With what?" I ask.

"It's still your birthday for a little while longer," she says.

"What do you have in mind?"

"Why don't you get in and get clean?"

I step out of my clothes and into the shower. She watches, biting her bottom lip as I wash my body. We step out together and grab towels.

"You're quiet," I say.

"Just thinking," she says.

"I never asked you how you were doing with all of this. It must be a shock."

"That's an understatement."

"I had no idea any of this would happen."

"I know. It was my fault. I shouldn't have been there. You were right."

"There's nothing we can do about that now. I'm glad I got to spend my birthday with you."

"Really?"

"Even though it turned into a disaster."

"We did have fun," she says.

"We did," I agree.

"We can still have some more," she says, her eyebrow raised.

I know exactly what she wants. "I have a better idea."

"What can be better than that?" she raises her eyebrow again.

"Why don't we slow it down?"

"How?" she asks.

I pull back the covers on my bed and lie down. Holding out my hand, I invite her to join me. She slides in next to me, pressing her back into my body as I wrap her in my arms.

"How did you turn into a wolf? Were you born that way?" she asks.

"Yes, I come from a long line of werewolves."

"So, your whole family?"

"All shifters," I say.

"What's a shifter?"

"Part human, part animal. We can transition, or shift, between the two parts of our being."

"Whenever you want?"

"Yes."

"This is some Hollywood movie shit," she says.

"Those stories come from somewhere, I suppose. Although, they don't do us justice."

"I know that now," she says.

"Were you afraid?" I ask.

"Not of you, never of you, Jeremiah."

That makes me feel good on the inside. "You handled it surprisingly well."

"My grandmother used to tell me stories about werewolves. I thought she just liked folklore."

I smile. "Your grandmother knew what I was the moment she saw me."

"She did?"

"Yes, I wasn't the first werewolf she'd met."

"I wish she would've told me."

"It's not something for public knowledge. I need you to keep this a secret. Can you do that?"

"Yes."

"Thank you."

"Where is your mother?"

"She died when I was a baby, and James acts like she never existed. He never talked about her."

"I'm sorry."

"I researched her background. Her name was Rachel Johnson. I know a lot of facts about her. I've seen pictures of her, but I don't know any real details about her, like her favorite color or if she was kind, or smart, or funny."

"I think she must've been a lovely person."

"Why do you say that?"

"The good parts of you had to come from somewhere. They sure as hell didn't come from your father. I think she's looking down on you, and she's proud of the man you've become."

I squeeze her.

"Is it okay for a shifter to be with someone like me?"

"A shifter would be lucky to be with someone like you." I kiss her neck. "Why don't you go to sleep, and we can talk more in the morning?"

"Okay," she says.

We drift off to sleep with her snuggled in my arms. I dream about her, about a life with her. One I've desperately been trying to avoid. I toss and turn until I awaken. My dick is still erect from my visions of her. I lie awake, staring at the ceiling with my hands behind my head.

Shante must've been sensitive to my movements because she stretches and yawns. "What time is it?" she asks.

"It's still dark. Go back to sleep," I say.

She sits up and looks at me. "I'm not sleepy anymore." She kisses me. I remove my hands from my head and place them in her hair. Her hair is so soft and smells like strawberries. She moans her delight until we pull apart.

"Thank you. Now, go back to sleep," I say.

I'm expecting some smart-ass reply, but she lets her body do the talking. She climbs on top of me. The look in her eyes tells me everything she's thinking. She rests her arms on my chest and leans over me. Her hair falls over her face, like in my fantasy.

"What are you doing?" I ask.

She slowly lowers herself onto my dick. Her pussy clenches me. I can't help but verbalize my pleasure as she engulfs me.

130

I sink my fingers into the plump flesh of her hips. "Ride this dick," I say as I pull her down to the base.

She cries out, and I hold on to her, grunting. I swear her pussy is magic. She rocks her hips, and the pleasure is so intense I have to bite my lip to keep from yelling. Her rhythm is slow and easy.

"Don't hold back," I say.

She bounces up and down. This shit feels so good. I can no longer fight the moans that escape my lips. I grab her breasts and squeeze as she rides me like a jet ski. She lowers herself, and I take her breast into my mouth, sucking her nipple.

I dig my fingers into her skin and thrust my hips to penetrate her as deep as she'll allow. She holds onto the headboard and yells with every move of my hips. My body goes wild as she tightens around me, screaming my name.

"That's right. Who's your alpha?" I smack her ass.

"Jeremiah B. Johnson, JD," she yells between ragged breaths.

"Motherfucking right," I say.

Her fingers claw my shoulders as she comes hard.

"I'm going to come with you, baby." I growl into her ear and pull out as I grunt while my nut shoots out like a rocket onto the bed. I massage my dick as the sensation leaves my body. She slides down and puts my dick in her mouth.

My body shivers as she sucks. "Damn, Shante." I play with her hair. I take a couple of deep breaths as she rises with a smile.

"Is my alpha happy?" She asks.

"Very pleased," I say.

"Good." She snuggles against my body.

"I told you to go back to sleep," I say as I wrap her in my arms.

"You know I have a problem doing what I'm told," she says.

"Since you're awake, I need you to do something for me."

"What?"

"I want you to stay here until things blow over. Can you do that?"

"Do you really think that's necessary?"

"I do. I need you to do what I tell you to do this time."

"Are you going to stay with me?"

"No. You'll have the place to yourself. We'll get some things from your apartment. I'm not going to hold you hostage. You can come and go as you please. I just want to make sure you have a safe place to come home to."

"Why can't you stay too?"

"I need to take care of some things, and I need to figure out some things. I need to be honest with you. Can you handle that?"

"Yes."

"I do care about you, but I don't know if I can give you everything you want right now."

"I'm not going to lie, that hurts."

"I know, and I hope you can forgive me. I just need some time. Can you give me that?"

"I can, but promise me you won't close the door on us."

"I won't."

"I'm going to be gone for the next couple of days. I probably won't see you until class on Monday. When I get back, we can talk."

"If you think it's best."

"I do."

"Where are you going?"

"Shante, I have business to attend to. Do you understand?"

"Yes," she says.

"Don't question me about it again," I warn her.

"Okay," she nods.

I kiss her lips.

"Get some rest, okay. Big Daddy will take you out for a big breakfast."

"Like a date?" she asks.

_____

132

"Sure, after we go get your things," I say.

"Okay. Can Big Daddy just hold me?"

"Of course." I squeeze her body tight until she falls asleep.

I awaken a short time later and just listen to her breathe. My mate lies next to me so close and yet so far. Her body still pressed against mine, I run my fingers along her skin and I'm swept with desire. My dick is hard and I position myself at her entrance. She moans and lifts her leg to accommodate me. I kiss and bite her back and squeeze her breasts as I enter her. She presses her body into mine and we make love. Our moans echo throughout the room as she comes over and over again.

XIII ~ Shante

It's been a couple of days. I haven't seen or heard from Jeremiah since his birthday. What a day that was. I've finally been able to acclimate to this big house. It's smaller than his main house but big enough for a family. I can't believe he wants me to stay here. Who does that?

But I agreed to it, so I go grocery shopping to get some of the things I like. Jeremiah offered me the use of one of his cars. While I'm living in this fantasy bubble, I may as well drive the luxury vehicle I could never afford.

Thanks to my grandmother, I have a little money in the bank now, but I'm using that for self-improvement, not frivolous purchases. Maybe I can afford one someday. I'm living amongst werewolves, shifters, and who knows what else, so anything is possible.

I'm so preoccupied, looking through the produce section that I don't notice I'm being watched. I jump when a hand grabs my shoulder. I've been through a lot lately, so my first instinct is to swing. I smack the man in the face.

"Strike," I yell. "What the hell? You can't sneak up on me like that." I pull my headphones from my ears.

"Sorry, I thought you heard me calling you. I didn't know you were throwing hands like that."

"You'd better watch out. I'm not playing around," I say.

"I see that. Although, you may want to work on your follow through. If you need to hit somebody, don't hesitate. Give it everything you've got."

"Noted," I say.

"How are you?" He asks me as I pick over the apples.

"I'm okay. I guess."

"I'm sorry we scared you the other night."

"I'll be alright."

"Don't put any of that on yourself. Our problems are our problems."

"I hope you can get past it. I hope you can at least have a relationship with your brother."

"My brother made it clear he wants nothing to do with me. It's something I have to live with, but I hope you don't feel the same way he does."

"Strike, I don't have any beef with you, but please don't involve me in your problems with your brother."

"I would never do that."

"Thank you."

"I meant what I said. I like you. I want you."

"I can't do that to Jeremiah," I say.

"What do you and Jeremiah have that's so special?"

"Let's not get into that."

"He hasn't mated you."

"What does that mean?"

"He hasn't even told you." He looks at me like I'm pathetic.

"Told me what."

"What kind of relationship do you two have?" he asks.

"Our relationship is none of your business, Strike."

"You are not some common, round the way girl, Shante. You're special, and if Jeremiah doesn't see that, you can do better."

135

"He and I are just fine. Our situation is unique. We're figuring it out."

"You don't know my brother like I do."

"I know him well," I say.

"If you were mine, I'd mate you. I wouldn't hesitate to make you mine. I wouldn't string you along like he's doing."

"That's not what he's doing. I don't like what you're implying."

"Game recognize game."

"Your brother is not like you. You don't understand."

"You don't understand what kind of man you're dealing with. He wants everything and everyone to be perfect, and if you don't fit his perfect image, he doesn't have room for you."

That's the thing I've worried about when it comes to Jeremiah. "Jeremiah has a good heart. He cares about people, and he cares about me. He's never done anything to make me think that."

"He's never tried to fix you or correct you? He reprimands people for fun. He's controlling."

"Stop it, Strike," I say as I look through the organic vegetables.

"Choose me."

I whip my head around. "You can't be serious."

"I can be the king, and you'll be my queen. We can run this city. You can have money, power. Anything you want."

"Why? You don't even know me."

"The moment I saw you, when you almost knocked me down in the hallway, I was yours." He touches my cheek. "You just didn't know it."

"You can have any woman you want."

"And I choose you."

He's playing mind games. This doesn't make sense to me. "I don't want to be a part of your game, okay. The last time I saw you, I was fucking your brother, and I loved it, every spine tingling second of it. I never came so hard in my life."

His jaw clenches, and his eyes fill with rage.

"You're telling me you're okay with that? Can you live a life with me with that image in your head?"

"I'm not like my brother. I'm a secure man. I won't hold your past against you."

"Yeah, right."

"I like you the way you are. Are you sure my brother can say the same?"

"I have to go."

"If he hasn't mated you, he has no intention of being with you."

"Thanks for the words of encouragement," I say as I walk off.

He grabs my arm.

I whip around and cut my eyes at him.

"Don't be mad at me. I want you to know you don't have to wait for him."

"That's enough," I yell.

"You'd rather chase after a man who doesn't want you than be with someone who's sure that he's crazy about you."

"I guess so." I challenge him with my eyes.

He grabs my arm and grips.

"Let me go."

He growls.

"This is a public place. I can cause a scene if I need to," I say.

"And I can take you." He shakes my arm and squeezes. "I can have you out of here before anyone notices you're gone. I can bring you home with me, and make you mine, and everything you feel for him, you'll feel for me."

"Get your hands off me. Nobody's taking me. Have you lost your mind?"

"Maybe I have."

"What's happening to you. I jerk my arm away."

137

"Why am I losing everything to my brother?"

"You never had me. I've always loved him."

"You prefer him. Our father prefers him. I'm tired of not being taken seriously. None of you know what I'm capable of."

"I'm sure you're very capable, but the person you need to convince is yourself."

"You have no idea." The look in his eyes scares me. Before I know it he grabs my arm again and takes off.

"Strike, let me go. What are you doing?"

"You're coming with me."

"I'm not. Let me go."

He keeps walking. "I'm going to show you how capable I am."

"Strike, do you really want to force me to be with you." I jerk my body, but his grip is too tight.

"I won't have to force you to do anything. You'll see."

"You're hurting me. You said you would never hurt me."

Strike shakes his head like he's breaking a trance. He looks at his hand and immediately loosens his grip on my arm. "I'm sorry Shante. I'm sorry."

Three guys run over to where we stand. One of them stands in front of me. "Are you okay?" he asks looking back at me.

I take a series of deep breaths. I'm shaken up, but I'll be fine. "I'm okay." I say to the man.

"What the fuck is wrong with you?" he asks Strike.

Strike throws his hands up and backs up.

"Bye, Shante."

"I don't reply."

"You're not going anywhere," one of the men says.

"We're in a public place," Strike says.

"I don't give a fuck. I know you didn't put your hands on this woman."

"It was a misunderstanding."

Strike turns to run and the guy grabs him before he can get away. He has quick reflexes. He holds Strike by the neck and he and the other guy drag him outside.

"What's happening?" I ask.

"They're going to make sure he doesn't bother you. Are you okay?" He touches my shoulder gently.

I flinch. "I think so. Are you guys security?"

He avoids my gaze. "Yes ma'am . We saw you on the cameras." He points to the ceiling.

I don't see any cameras. I guess they're hidden. They'd have to be pretty strong to take control of Strike. He's a shifter. I wonder if they're shifters too.

"Thank you."

"No problem, ma'am."

Strike was cute and charming, but I don't recognize him anymore. I don't know if he followed me here or what. He's making me nervous, and I don't know if I should tell Jeremiah or not. I think Jeremiah would kill him. Maybe he deserves it.

He has me spooked. I keep looking around. I can't have Strike or anyone else sneaking up on me again. I wish Jeremiah was here with me. I feel safer when he's around.

"My name is Marcus," the man says.

"Thank you, Marcus."

"Would you like me to walk with you to your car?"

"No thank you. I'll be fine."

"If you're sure."

"I'm sure. I have a few more things to get."

"Okay, I'll keep an eye on you." He points to the ceiling.

"Bye."

Marcus seems like a good guy, but I don't know who to trust or what to think anymore. I quickly make my way through the store and leave.

XIV ~ Jeremiah

I'm sitting at home when the doorbell rings. My brother's scent invades my nose.

"Where's Shante?" he asks as we walk into the living room.

"You don't need to concern yourself with Shante."

"Somebody should be concerned about her."

"What the fuck is that supposed to mean?"

"I was talking to her."

I turn around. "When?" My nostrils flare.

"I ran into her at the store. Seems to me like you don't appreciate her like you should. If she were my woman, I'd treat her like a queen. She wouldn't have to question her place in my life."

I punch him in the face, breaking his nose.

He pushes my chest. "You don't deserve her." He yells as he pushes his nose back into place.

I grab his neck and carry him outside to the back yard. I want to kill him, but I'm not about to mess up my house. Words can't describe the wrath I feel.

I punch him again and push him into the side of the house. "Motherfucker." I swing again.

He ducks causing me to hit the brick. "Shit," I yell as I shake my hand off.

William takes the opportunity to hit me in the stomach. I double over and he uppercuts me.

"I see you finally learned a few moves little brother," I say as I lift myself up.

"You don't know me," he says.

We circle one another.

"Were those your guys?" he asks me.

"You motherfucking right. You're lucky I was out of town. You'd be a dead man." I swing.

He leans back. "Too slow old man."

"I'm about to show you what an old man can do." I crack my knuckles. "Not only did you approach Shante, you put your filthy hands on her." I swing and he moves his head to the side. I missed on purpose.

"Don't get mad at me because you can't appreciate a good woman."

"Don't you ever talk to me or anybody else about Shante. What she and I do is none of your business."

I swing for him, this time landing a blow to his jaw. Then I go in. "You put your hands on my mate. I should kill you."

Blood covers my hands. It's not mine. It's his. He throws his hands up to block my hits.

"Look at you. You want to be an alpha. You want someone to give you a pack? Are you serious? You can't even defend yourself." I punch him again.

"You sound just like your father," he says. "He was right. You're just like him."

I tackle him to the ground and beat his ass.

"You stay the fuck away from her or I swear I'll kill you." I know the guys I had watching Shante already taught him a lesson, but just to make my point I grab his arm and twist it back until it breaks.

He cries out in pain. I can only imagine it's excruciating. "Stop," he yells, "please. Get off me," he yells. "I'm sorry."

"You are a sorry ass excuse for a man." I break his arm in another place before I let him go. I pace back and forth to calm my wolf and give him time to heal.

"I know I deserved that. I apologized to Shante. I don't know what came over me."

"I don't care. There's no excuse."

"You're right. You know that's not me. I'll stay away from her."

"You'd better. Now what are you doing here? I know you didn't come to talk about Shante."

"Once again, your father has sent me to talk to you."

"You're not tired of being his errand boy yet? What does the old man want now?"

"He wants what he wanted before. He wants you to take over his pack."

"Is that what you want?"

"I want what he wants. I'm here on his behalf. I have no say in this."

"And what will happen to you. I thought you wanted his pack."

"I'll be your beta."

"Are you suddenly okay with that?"

"I'm used to being second best."

"You're not even a beta. You have so much to learn. I have no use for you, William."

"You're so wise, aren't you? You're so much better than the rest of us."

"I want to know why he suddenly wants me to take over?"

"You're the golden boy. You have clout and respect amongst powerful people. You can go places he and I can't."

"He knows that I would never use those connections for him."

"Maybe you'll change your mind."

"That will never happen. Which of these connections does he need right now?"

"He hasn't told me, but I've heard things."

"What kind of things?"

"Rumor has it that The Alliance is making changes. Members are being ousted, and our father feels like he might be one of them."

"What makes him think that?"

"Let's just say these members have questionable morals."

"What does that have to do with me?"

"Don't you think you'd fit in perfectly?"

"How should I know?"

"You work for the man in charge."

"I have nothing to do with The Alliance."

"Preston Jacobs has taken over The Alliance, and he wants a cleaner image. You, brother, are squeaky clean. If he gives you the pack you can infiltrate The Alliance."

"I'll consider his offer." Not for the reasons James wants. If I were to take over my that man's pack, I'd never allow any illegal activity. James has to know that, which leads me to believe that he would be running things behind my back.

"You'll be alpha. It's all yours. He does have one condition."

"What's that?"

"You can't be with Shante."

"There's no way I'd agree to that."

"So, you do love her?"

"Keep her name out of your mouth."

"He believes you need a mate that can add value to the pack. His exact words were, you can fuck her, but you can't mate her. She's nobody."

"Tell him he can go to hell. I'm not interested. The pack is all yours, baby brother."

"Maybe you should reconsider," he says.

"You want me to reconsider because you think you'll have a shot at Shante. Let me tell you something. Shante knows what she wants. I'm sorry your little feelings are hurt, but she'll never want you. I think you saw that for yourself."

"He won't be happy. You know that."

"Tell him he can come see me, man to man, alpha to alpha. I promise I won't let him go again. He should be thankful that Shante saved his pathetic excuse for a life. It's time for you to go, brother."

"Fine. Thanks for nothing."

"You can see yourself out through the side gate. You're not welcome in my home again." If William were not my brother, I'd be dragging him out and burying his body.

XV ~ Shante

"Hello, can you tell me where Jeremiah Johnson's office is?"

"I don't think so."

"I'm sorry. Why not?"

"Who are you?"

"I'm here to see Jeremiah Johnson."

"Do you have an appointment?"

"Yes," I lie. The guy at the information desk at Alpha Security Corporation isn't too friendly, and he doesn't seem to want to tell me where to find Jeremiah. I sigh. I was hoping to surprise him, but I don't think I can get into this big, fancy building.

He looks at his tablet and presses some buttons. "I need to see your ID."

"Why?"

"Miss, you can't walk in here unannounced. We need to know who's in this building and why."

"Sorry, I'm here to see Jeremiah. It's kind of a surprise." I look to him, hoping he'll see I'm not crazy, and he'll give me one of those black and white visitor badges I see in front of him.

"Unfortunately, I can't let you in without an appointment."

"Can you call him?"

"I can't do that, ma'am."

"I promise he won't be upset."

"That's not how things work here, ma'am. You'll have to make an appointment. Now, if you'll excuse me."

"Tell Jeremiah Johnson Shante is here. He'll want to see me."

"What's going on here?" I hear a woman's voice behind me.

"Hello, Mrs. Jacobs, Mr. Jacobs. Nothing for you to worry about."

"Do I smell oxtails?" The woman asks.

"How do you know that?" I turn around, and a beautiful pregnant woman is standing behind me with a man. She has gorgeous curly hair and glowing skin, not to mention an incredible fashion sense. She's wearing heels while pregnant and this cute blue dress. The man she's with is tall, dark, and sexy as hell, wearing an expensive black suit, and his eyes are mesmerizing, almost like Jeremiah's. They're holding hands. Looking at them makes me think of a future with Jeremiah.

"The babies love oxtails," she says, smiling at me.

"Babies?"

"Triplets."

"Triplets? Are you serious?"

"Samantha, let the man do his job," the man says.

"I am."

"Come on, let's go," he says with his deep, velvety voice.

"Wait. You're looking for Jeremiah?" she asks me.

"I am. Do you know him?" I ask.

"You brought him food?" Samantha asks.

"Yes," I say.

"Come with me," she says.

"Really?" I ask.

"No," the man says. He's firm. He reminds me so much of Jeremiah.

"Yes," Samantha says.

"Sam, you don't even know what you're getting involved in. If he wanted her here, he would've given her access."

"Maybe he hasn't had a chance. I know they belong together, Preston."

"You don't know that," Preston says.

"Baby, she loves him. I'm telling you. They belong together." She looks at me. "I have a knack for this."

"Even if that's true, and I'm not convinced that it is, it's still none of your business," Preston says.

"I want to talk to her. Can she come with us, please?" She bats her eyelashes.

Preston sighs. He kisses Sam on the cheek. "We got it from here," he says to the man behind the desk.

"Yes, sir." The man hands me a visitor badge.

"Shante, come with me," Samantha says.

"What just happened?" I ask as I follow Samantha and Preston through the turnstile and to the elevator.

"What happened is my wife is going to get involved in your personal life after I tell her to mind her own business," Preston says.

"I'm sorry. I wasn't trying to cause any problems. I just wanted to surprise Jeremiah with lunch."

"It's fine. My handsome husband is exaggerating. I'm just going to take you to Jeremiah."

He wraps his arms around his wife, placing his hands on her stomach. "Sure, you are."

"You think you know everything, don't you?"

"I know everything I need to know about you." He kisses her forehead.

"We're just going to take her to Jeremiah. That's all."

"Who are you people?" I ask as the elevator climbs.

"Preston Jacobs. This is my building."

"Are you Jeremiah's boss?"

"Yes, I am."

147

"This is my mate, Samantha."

"Your mate?" I ask.

"Yes, my husband," Samantha says.

"Jeremiah used those words before. What exactly do you mean?"

"I knew it," Samantha says.

"Sam, stop it. It means we're partners for life," Preston says.

"There must be more to it," I say. My mind replays everything that happened with Jeremiah in the beginning. He called me his mate. Strike said he would make me his mate.

"It's something you and Jeremiah should discuss," Preston says.

"Maybe it's something you and I should discuss," Samantha says to me. "Call me, Sam." She extends her hand, and I shake it.

"Sam, nice to meet you both. You two are relationship goals. I am here for this. All of it."

"Thanks, girl. I got a good man. You do too."

"He is a good man. We have some things to work out, though."

"Samantha and I will allow you to work through them. Won't we, Sam?"

"Of course," she says.

"You're so serious, just like Jeremiah. He rarely smiles," I say to Preston.

"We're busy," Preston says.

"Does that mean you can't laugh?"

"That means they're so worried about the people they care about and the women they love, they forget to enjoy life sometimes. That's why they have us." She looks into his eyes, and the love between them almost brings tears to my eyes.

The elevator stops, and the doors open. They're still staring at one another.

"I'll take her and meet you upstairs," Sam says to Preston.

"Be good, ladies." He holds the elevator door as we walk out.

"We will."

"Thank you, Mr. Jacobs."

He nods as the door closes.

"How did you get that man?" I ask Sam.

She points. "It all started with a look in that elevator."

"Was it love at first sight?"

"For him, yes. It may have been for me, but I was so busy yelling at him, I missed it."

"I need to hear about this."

She laughs. "Follow me. My palms were sweaty, and my heart was racing, but I was so mad at his sexy ass, I forgot about all that."

"Sounds like the first time I saw Jeremiah. I was so pissed at him. My mouth got me in trouble. He was so mad at me, he picked me up and carried me outside."

"A woman after my own heart."

We walk through the contemporary office space. The people are polished and poised, and the decor is trendy. "This building is beautiful," I say.

"That's Preston's doing. The first time I stepped in those doors, I knew I wanted to work here," Sam says.

"You work here, too."

"I was applying for a job when I met Preston."

"Talk about a power couple."

"This is it."

I stare at the door with Jeremiah's name on the outside. "How do I look?"

"Gorgeous," Sam says. She knocks on the door.

"One moment," Jeremiah says from the other side. My heart races.

"It's okay. Be cool," Sam says, touching my arm.

The door opens. Jeremiah is wearing a black sweater vest over a white shirt with a red tie and black slacks. "Shante."

"Hi," I say.

"What are you doing here?" he asks.

———
149

"I found her wandering the halls looking for you," Sam says.

Jeremiah does not look happy, but he does look sexy. There goes that vein.

"Surprise," I say.

"Thank you for bringing her to me, Sam."

"No problem. You're a lucky man."

"I am," Jeremiah says.

I feel like a little girl who's going to be in trouble as soon as company leaves.

"I'll see you later, Shante," Sam says.

"Thanks, Sam."

"Come in," Jeremiah says. He closes the door behind me.

"I brought you lunch."

"This is my job, Shante." He grits his teeth.

"I know."

"What are you doing here?"

"I wanted to talk to you."

"You thought it was a good idea to come to my job?"

"I didn't think you would mind."

"You surprise me in my classroom. You pop up at my office. You follow me to the woods, and now, you show up here. What are you thinking?"

"I was trying to do something nice."

"I told you I need time. You have to stop this. What's wrong with you?"

"Nothing is wrong with me. What's your problem?"

"My problem is I spent a lot of time trying to forget about you, and you keep inserting yourself into my life like nothing happened."

"That's an overreaction."

"How do I get to react? You tell me."

"You act like I didn't get hurt too. You made love to me, and then you bulldozed me."

"How did I bulldoze you?"

"All your talk about being on the same page. You knew we were not on the same page. You knew I had

---

150

feelings for you. You hurt me on purpose. I wouldn't do that to you."

"You're the one who jumped on my dick. I didn't ask for any of this."

"You didn't stop it either."

"How did you even get in here?"

"Sam let me in."

"How do you know Sam?"

"We just met."

He walks to the giant window in his office. I swear you can see the whole city from here.

I sit the food on a table and step behind him. "Why are you mad at me? I thought we were in a better place."

"It's too much, Shante. You can't keep popping up everywhere. I'm trying to be nice to you, but you can't do this. This is my job, how I make a living. I've accepted that you're in my class. That's not enough for you?"

"No. It's not enough. I'm more than just a student, and you know it. Look at me," I yell.

He faces me.

"You know what we have is more than that. I'm tired of you trying to push me away. I'm not the one with the problem. So what, you've accepted me as a student. Have you accepted me as your mate?"

"What did you say?"

"Have you accepted me as your mate?"

"Where did you hear this?"

"From you. The first time we kissed. Do you remember? Preston said Sam is his mate. It reminded me of what you said to me."

"You shouldn't be here."

"Come to me, my mate." I step closer and grab his hand.

His eyes change colors.

"There's a part of you that wants to be with me, and you try not to give in, but you can't resist. Can you?"

"That part is my wolf, but he's not in charge. I am. I gave in before. I won't do it again."

151

"You're mad because your feelings got hurt one time. You know who's tired? Me. I'm tired of you pushing me around. You keep holding that one moment over my head, and I feel terrible about it, but I'm done apologizing. Yeah, I said I didn't want you, but it's not all my fault, and you know I didn't mean it, and I'm tired of you punishing me. I was hurt that day too. All you think about is yourself."

He touches my shoulder. "Take your hand off me. You can't keep doing this to me. I'm a good woman, and I know it, and if you can't see that, maybe Strike can."

He grabs my arm. "You will not threaten me with him."

"I don't have to threaten you. Strike knows what he wants."

"You told me nothing was going on with you two."

"Take your hands off me."

"Now you're creeping around with him in the produce aisle?"

"Are you following me?"

"What were you two talking about?"

"You have no right?"

"I have every right to make sure you're safe. I told you to stay away from him. Didn't I?"

"I have no control over where he goes. I didn't invite him to the public grocery store. How is it my fault he showed up there? Is that why you're mad at me? Seriously?"

"You don't listen. You don't think."

"I'm sick of you," I yell.

I storm out of his office and slam the door. I jump when I see Sam standing there.

"Not the reaction you were hoping for, I take it," Sam says.

"You almost gave me a heart attack. What are you doing out here?"

"That was tragic."

"You heard us?"

"Yes.

152

"How?"

She ignores me. "We need to fix this. Jeremiah knows you're his mate, but he's being stubborn. Come with me, and tell me exactly what happened."

"First, can you tell me about mating?"

"I was like you, human, and I fell in love with a wolf shifter."

"Preston's a wolf too," I say. "That makes sense."

"He and Jeremiah are alphas. They're strong, masculine, and they're proud."

"Shifters mate for life. They're aware that someday they're going to meet their fated mates. That is the person they're destined to be with. When a shifter finds their mate, they instantly know it. If a shifter's fated mate is human—"

"The shifter knows, but the human doesn't," I say.

"Right," Sam says. "If you're like me, you felt something, but you didn't know what it was or why you were so drawn to him. Jeremiah has been fighting his feelings for you as you suspected."

"His brother said what we have isn't real because he hasn't mated me yet. How would he mate me?"

"He'd mark you."

I flinch when Sam lifts my skirt.

She nods at the scratch marks on my thigh. "Like that."

"I had no idea what that was. I thought he was just lost in the moment."

"I'm sure he was. The most important thing is the bite." She tilts her head to the side and shows me her neck where her bite marks have healed.

"What happens when he bites you?"

"The most incredible feeling you will ever experience. Then you'll bite him in the same manner."

"How?"

"That's when the change happens."

"That's how you became a wolf shifter?" I ask.

"Yes."

153

"How did you feel?"

"My shift took a while, so I didn't feel different right away, but it took a little time to get used to it."

"Do you regret it?"

"No. I'm stronger, my body heals faster, and I'm connected to my mate. What we share can hardly be put into words. It's like I'm a part of him, and he's part of me. We have a unique bond."

"Should I be scared?"

"No, you should be excited, that is, if Jeremiah gets his head out of his ass."

"This situation has been hard on both of us."

I follow Sam into her office on the top floor. This whole time Jeremiah knew I was his mate, and he's been resisting me. She sits at her desk. I sit in a chair across from her and give her a condensed version of what happened between Jeremiah and me.

"Preston," Sam calls.

It takes a moment for him to step outside his office. "Yes?" He walks over to Sam.

"Did you hear what she said?"

"Unfortunately."

"What do you think?" Sam asks.

"If I was him, I would've never talked to you again."

"Really? That bad? Even if she's his mate?"

"A good man's instinct is to protect and love you. When you have a mate, every part of his being is invested in you. What he feels for you is stronger than anything he's ever felt. He protected you, and you stomped on his heart. An apology doesn't make that betrayal go away."

"I apologized for hurting him, but I've also been working my ass off here."

"What can she do?"

"She and Jeremiah can work this out themselves."

"Preston, come on. Can you honestly tell me if that were you and me, you would've done me like that?"

"Look, he's a proud man. He doesn't like to lose. You're lucky he's even talking to you. Use that to your advantage."

"I'm trying to."

"Throwing yourself at him is not the answer. He's an alpha. Women have been doing that his whole life."

"I'm not throwing myself at him. I'm trying to make amends. I'm trying to get him back."

"It comes across as desperate."

"Preston," Sam reprimands him.

"It's okay. I appreciate you telling it like it is. I don't want to appear desperate, but I love him. I want to be with him."

"You sound desperate," they say in unison.

"Damnit," I say. "I can work on that. Thank you, both."

"I have an idea," Sam says.

"No, my sweet, you have work to do, and that includes not getting involved."

Sam pulls out her phone. "You're having lunch with me," she says to me. She turns to Preston. "Why don't you talk to Jeremiah? See if you can nudge him in the right direction."

"Because I believe they should work it out themselves."

"But you do agree they should work it out."

"I hope they do."

"Get him talking and tell him that. A little nudge from someone he respects may help him get over himself."

"I'm staying out of it."

"Preston, do it for love."

"You're all the love I need."

"Do it for me."

"You need to stay out of it, too."

"Do it for the babies."

"This has nothing to do with the babies."

"It would make us happy." Sam rubs her belly and gives him puppy dog eyes.

155

Preston sighs.

"Thank you, Alpha." Sam smiles big and bright.

Preston helps Sam out of her chair. "I didn't say I was doing it."

"I know," Sam says.

"Where are we going?" I ask.

"We're going to have some girl talk. I'll be back," she says to Preston.

"Come here," he says.

She grabs his hands.

He pulls her close and kisses her lips. "I love you." His hands rub her stomach.

"I love you, too."

They kiss some more.

I clear my throat. "Excuse me. I'm a little bitter right now. This isn't helping."

Sam laughs. "We'll get you there. Let's go."

XVI ~ Jeremiah

"Jeremiah," Preston says as I walk into his office.

"Gentlemen," I say.

"Come in. Have a seat," Preston says. He's sitting on one of the black leather couches in his office with Michael, his second in command. They're the only two people I answer to at ASC. Preston is CEO, and Michael is COO.

"Sam texted and said you wanted to see me. I went ahead and brought some contracts for you to sign." I hand Preston the contracts.

"She did?" Preston accepts them.

"Yes, but she's not at her desk," I say.

"She's having lunch with her girls," Preston says.

"That means she'll be taking the rest of the day off," Michael says.

"How's everything going with The Red Woods Pack?" I ask Michael.

Michael leans back and scratches his beard. "It's an adjustment, but so far, so good." Michael looks different now that he's alpha of his own pack. His usual easygoing vibe is a bit more serious.

"I would imagine, but if you need help or anything, I got you," I say.

"Me too, brother," Preston says.

"Oh, yeah. You have King Alpha at your disposal," I say.

Michael laughs.

"You're joking, but I like the sound of that," Preston says.

"Thanks, guys. I'll keep that in mind," Michael says.

"Why'd you want to see me?" I ask Preston.

"I didn't," Preston says.

"Why did Sam text me?"

"She met your mate," Preston says.

"My what?" I ask.

"You have a mate?" Michael asks.

"No," I say.

"Shante was here, trying to get in the building."

"I hope you won't hold it against me," I say.

"It's fine. She certainly is spirited."

"She's driving me crazy."

"Sam is convinced you two belong together," Preston says.

Michael smirks. "That means she won't rest until you mate."

"Why does she care?" I ask.

"She loves love, and even though her enthusiasm works my nerves, her eyes light up when she thinks she can bring people together. I don't want her to lose that."

Michael and I look at one another, then at Preston.

"What?" he asks.

"She has you wrapped around her finger, and when those babies come, it's a wrap," Michael says.

"That's not true, and need I remind you that you were chasing Lisa all over the city, begging her to give you another chance," Preston says to Michael.

"It worked," Michael says.

"I remember you begging at the wedding," I say, laughing.

"And you," Preston points to me. "Come to me, my mate."

"How do you know that?"

"The women were talking. I know everything," Preston says.

Anger rises in me.

"Calm down," Preston says. "Don't be so hard on Shante."

"I've been nothing but nice to her."

"You've been using her. That's not fair to her."

"What did you say to me?"

"She makes you feel good about yourself, so you keep her around."

"I'm not using her. She's been following me, and dropping in on me, and popping up at my job. I haven't encouraged her behavior at all. She won't stop."

"You slept with her... again. What did you think would happen?" Preston asks.

"You don't know what you're talking about. And frankly, it's none of your damn business."

"I know it's none of my business. I'd rather not know any details, but your girlfriend came to my building with lunch for you, and my mate is now invested in your situation. If you had taken care of your business, I'd still be blissfully ignorant."

I stand, pointing my finger at Preston. "That doesn't give you the right to throw out accusations. Nobody asked for your opinion."

Preston stands and advances toward me. "Shante asked for my opinion."

"Keep her name out of your mouth," I say through clenched teeth. I step toward him. I'll fight him if I have to.

"Or what?" Preston says. "She's not your mate. You don't even want her."

Michael jumps up and inserts himself between us. "What the hell is wrong with you two? You are not about to fight in the office in the middle of the day? Sit down."

Preston folds his arms.

159

I forgot I was at work for a moment. "My apologies. I'm going to go." I walk off.

"Wait," Michael says.

I pause.

"Are you hungry?" he asks.

I think about the food Shante brought for me. She stormed out of my office without taking it. "As Preston pointed out, my girlfriend brought me lunch."

"Eat it for dinner. You look like you need a drink. Come with us," Michael says.

"I don't think so."

"Come," Preston says.

"Preston's buying," Michael says.

"Fine. I'm having the biggest lobster in the tank."

"Good luck. They don't have lobster," Preston says.

A car takes us to PJ's, a local bar where shifters hang out. I come here from time to time after work. Percy and his brothers built this place with their own hands. Everything is made of the same oak wood, and it's nicely constructed. When we walk through the door, I see Percy behind the bar with a man our age. They're arguing.

"Dad, what's going on here?" Preston says.

"Wade thinks he can teach me something about mixology. Can you believe that, son?" He looks at Wade. "I told him I've been doing this since he was a baby."

"I told him he needs to learn some new tricks. Times have changed. He needs to step his game up to attract more customers."

"A classic will always be a classic," Percy says.

"Classics are constantly remade and improved," Wade says.

Percy turns to us. "Hi, fellas."

"Percy, good to see you," I say.

"Good to see you, too, son," he says.

Wade turns to me. "Who is this?"

"Jeremiah," I say, extending my hand. "Nice to meet you."

"Nice sweater," he says as he shakes my hand.

"Thanks," I say. Wade is not like the rest of us. His clothes are casual, and he has a carefree vibe. He's tall and muscular like the rest of us. He's a shifter, but I don't know what kind.

"Wade is my beta," Preston says.

"What are you?" I ask.

"That's an offensive question," Wade says.

"Right now, he's a pain in my ass," Percy says.

"He's an immature, reckless dragon shifter," Michael says.

"At your service," Wade says.

Michael rolls his eyes.

"How is that possible? I thought dragons were extinct."

"It's a long story, one I'm still trying to figure out."

"I'd love to hear more."

Wade looks uncomfortable. "Some other time. What can I get you all to drink?" Wade asks.

"You can get from behind my bar," Percy says, swatting Wade with a towel.

We take our seats.

"Do you boys want some burgers?" Percy asks.

"Yes, please," we all say.

"Drinks?" Percy asks.

"You have that scotch I like?" Preston asks.

"Sure do."

"I'll have some of that too," I say.

"So, how's your mate, Jeremiah?" Percy asks while getting four glasses.

I sigh.

"It's a sore subject for him," Preston says.

"After all this time, you're still trying to fight your feelings for that young lady?" Percy says.

"How do you know about that?" Preston asks.

"I ran into Jeremiah a while back."

I take a gulp of my scotch.

"Jeremiah, I wanted to talk to you about The Alliance," Preston says.

I'm grateful to Preston for changing the subject. "What about it?"

"Why aren't you a member?"

We have now entered another subject I'm uncomfortable about. "The Alliance has never been a part of my plan."

"I can assure you, things are changing for the better. I'm in charge now, and we could use a guy like you," Preston says.

"Why's that?"

"I like what you're doing. You've taken on molding the next generation of wolf shifters. You and your leaders mentor them and shape them into our future leaders. It's admirable. The Alliance could use your influence," Preston says.

"How do you know all of this?" I ask.

"I'm good at what I do," Preston says.

"I'm not interested, but I appreciate it."

"You can't avoid him forever. If your father is an issue—"

"I don't want to talk about it," I interrupt him.

"I'm on your side. I'd be willing to negotiate," Preston says.

I do love a good negotiation, but I don't like that Preston is digging around in my business, but I created the contracts. I know he has every right to do so. I nod. I don't care to talk about it anymore.

"Let's change the subject. What happened with this woman of yours?" Michael asks.

"It's a long story."

"I see," Percy says. "You're as stubborn as my son. You're in love with that young lady, and you need her as much as she needs you."

"I was free of her, and all of a sudden, she shows up in my classroom this semester."

"It's time for you to let it go," Percy says. "Ask these three. Their lives are better with their mates. Isn't that right, boys?"

"I'm happy my mate is talking to me at all," Michael says.

"My mate wants to get married in a passive aggressive way," Wade says.

"Why don't you want to get married?" I ask.

"You sound like her," Wade says.

"What about you?" I ask Preston.

"My mate is perfect," Preston says.

"What's wrong with your girl? She got a butter face?" Wade asks me.

Michael spits out some of his drink.

"What?" Preston asks.

"A butter face, everything looks good, but her face," Wade says.

"Hell no, she's not a butter face," I say.

"Well, what's the problem? She got a lazy eye? Is she a gold digger? Is she a hoe?" Wade asks.

"I will kick your dragon ass across this bar," I say.

"What is wrong with you?" Michael asks Wade.

"Wade, show some respect," Percy says.

"I'm trying to figure it out. I thought I was the commitment phobic one in the group, but I've claimed my mate. I can't imagine you're more fucked up than me. There must be something wrong with her. What is it?"

"There's nothing wrong with her," Preston says. "She's beautiful. She's friendly, and she cooks."

My wolf growls.

"Relax, I have no interest in your little mate," Preston says.

"Yes, Preston only has eyes for the queen of his heart, the apple of his eye, the lovely Samantha Jacobs." Michael throws his hands in the air like he's in a Shakespeare play. He and Wade laugh.

Preston throws a balled-up napkin at Michael's head.

"What does she look like?" Michael asks.

I pull out my phone and open my photos. "This is her." I show Michael the photo of me and Shante.

"She's beautiful, and you look happy. You don't want her, but you keep a photo of you and her on your phone. This isn't social media. You saved this."

"I forgot to delete it."

"Let me see." Wade gets up and grabs the phone from Michael.

"'She's a dime, and you're tripping,'" Wade says.

"Give me my damn phone," I say. "Can I get another drink, please?"

Percy nods.

"Damn," Wade shouts. "I like this one."

I growl and reach for my phone. I know what photo he's looking at. He holds the phone back.

"I will kill you," I say.

Wade hands the phone to Preston, who looks and hands it to Michael.

I punch Wade in the stomach. He growls. His growl is different from ours, louder. I wonder if I'm about to see the dragon, and he bursts out laughing. "It was worth it," he says.

Michael hands me my phone.

"Forget you saw that," I say to them.

"That's sexy. I wonder if Lisa will pose on a motorcycle for me?" Michael says. "Maybe naked."

I growl.

"You sure are possessive for someone who doesn't even want your mate?" Preston says. "Do you plan to fight anyone who mentions her name?"

"That picture was not for your eyes," I say.

"Why do you still have it?" Wade asks. "There are only two photos saved to your phone, and both of them are of her."

"I don't use the camera. I forgot to delete them," I say.

"No time like the present. Delete them now," Percy says.

"I—"

"He can't," Preston says.

"Man, what did she do to you?" Wade asks.

"I heard her side of the story. Why don't you tell us what happened?" Preston says.

After a bit of reluctance, and after determining I'd be mocked regardless, I tell the guys what happened.

"That's fucked up," Wade says.

"I know," I say.

"I mean you," Wade says.

"What?"

"Are you going to punish her for the rest of your life? You know women are emotional."

"No, my goal was to stay away from her."

Preston talks. "I know why you're upset. I even told her I would've done the same thing, but you slept with her, and she's in your life now. I think you should at least try to work it out."

"I know what she's going through," Michael says. "Put yourself in her shoes. It was one reckless moment where she was careless with her words."

"Plus, you're to blame too," Wade says.

"How?"

"She had a boyfriend, and you knew that. How was she supposed to react when he walked in on his girl with you?"

"Fuck you," I say.

"Let that be the last time you talk to me like that," Wade says. I see fire in his eyes.

"I'm not scared of you," I say.

"Well, let's step outside, and I'll fight you for your girl. It's obvious you think you're better than her. If I beat your ass, she can come home with me. I know what to do with her."

I jump out of my chair and lunge for him. Preston stops me mid lunge with a chokehold.

"Don't hold him back," Wade says.

"Yeah, I think he can kick Wade's ass. Somebody needs to," Michael says.

"Wade, stand down," Preston yells.

165

"Boys, you are not going to tear up my bar. I'll kick all of your asses," Percy shouts.

Everyone turns their attention to Percy.

"Don't let the old age fool you. I still got some ass whippings left in me," Percy says. His face is serious. The alpha he usually suppresses is showing. Everyone looks startled. No one knows what to say. They say Percy was a beast in his day.

Suddenly, we all erupt in laughter, and everyone returns to their seats.

"Forgive us, Dad," Preston says.

"Don't be so hard on Jeremiah. He has every right to be hurt," Percy says.

"I didn't say I was hurt," I say.

"You didn't have to. You put yourself out there. You put it all on the line, and she broke your heart. Alpha's hurt deeper than anyone could ever know, but we're expected to be hard, strong at all times. It's okay to hurt. It's also okay to forgive. We all need forgiveness at some point in our lives," Percy says. He reaches across the bar and pats my shoulder before he walks off, leaving me with my thoughts.

I wish I had a father like Percy. Preston is lucky.

"He makes a good point," Michael says.

"I know, but it's more than that. Every time I come close to mating her, something happens. I don't want to be hurt, but I don't want her to get hurt either."

"I understand," Preston says. "You'll never stop worrying about your mate, but you can protect her, and you can teach her to protect herself. It'll be okay."

"Can we talk about something else?" I ask.

"Was that your bike in the picture?" Michael asks.

"Yeah, that's my baby."

"I was thinking about getting one," Michael says.

I'm relieved the subject has changed. The guys are so busy talking motorcycles and fast cars the subject of Shante doesn't come up again, and I actually have a good time. I can even tolerate Wade.

XVII ~ Shante

A town car takes us to Blue, the nicest restaurant downtown. I've only dreamt about going here. It's so exclusive that even if you do manage to get a reservation, they won't let you in. I can't help but be wide-eyed and in awe when we walk right inside. The lights are dim. It looks like money. I feel out of place, but you'd better believe I'm going to enjoy this shit.

The host immediately runs to Sam. "Well, if it isn't Mrs. Jacobs in all her glory. Look at you. You better show them how it's done, honey." He gives her two air kisses. I've never seen that in real life.

"Phillip, you're so crazy."

"How are the royal babies, darling?"

"They're healthy, kicking up a storm in there."

"Fabulous, and where is that husband of yours? You know I could always use some eye candy around here."

"It's just us girls today. I'll tell him you asked about him."

"Yes, please do," Phillip fans himself.

"Alright, now, don't be lusting over my man."

"I can't make any promises." They laugh.

"Who do we have here?" Phillip asks.

"This is my friend, Shante."

"Well, enchanté, Miss Shante."

"Very nice to meet you," I say.

"Likewise." He holds my hands and examines me. I'm not sure what he's doing. "I see you have on your catch a man skirt and heels. I am not mad at you."

"I does what I can," I laugh.

"And you does it well. Let me show you to your private table. The rest of your party has already arrived." Phillip leads us to a secluded table next to a huge window facing a beautiful garden with a fountain.

I swear the wait staff is wearing formal wear. This place is fancy, from the linens to the huge selection of silverware. I'm intimidated, but I remember seeing something that said work your way from the outside in with the utensils. I also remember I should sit my napkin in my lap as soon as I'm seated. Now, if I can remember to keep my elbows off the table, I'll be good.

Sam is excited to see her friends. They squeal and hug, give out compliments, and rub the belly before taking their seats.

"I didn't expect a party," I say.

"We need all hands on deck for your situation."

"What's her situation?" one of the women asks. She's tall, has shoulder length black hair and beautiful cocoa skin.

"Shante, this is my girl squad, Lisa," she points to the woman with the black hair, "and Simone," she points to the other, equally stunning, curvy woman with caramel skin and honey blonde hair. These women look like class and money. I need to step my game up.

"Nice to meet you both." I shake their hands. "I'm not exactly sure what's going on here."

"We're here to strategize. You're going to get your man back," Sam says.

"What happened," Lisa asks.

Sam and I tell the ladies about my dilemma. We order drinks and appetizers. They go through stages of amusement, shock, warm and fuzzies, and anger, everything I've experienced since meeting Jeremiah.

"He defended you," Simone says.

"He rescued you," Lisa says.

"He declared his love for you," Sam says.

"He came to your Nana's funeral," Simone says with her hands over her heart.

"He sounds like a good man," Lisa says.

"Why did you say that to him? He didn't deserve that," Simone says.

"I beat myself up for it every day. I don't know. I was," I bow my head, "ashamed, and I lashed out at him. I thought if that's how Brian saw me, Jeremiah would see me that way too. I couldn't even pick myself up off the floor after he left. I cried and cried, curled up in his jacket. I still have it."

"Poor thing," Sam says.

"How was the sex?" Lisa asks.

I'm not sharing the details, but I can't contain the smile forming on my lips.

"I know what that look means," Simone says.

I cover my face.

"Good enough for her to show up unannounced at his job with homemade oxtails and gravy, macaroni and cheese, greens, and sweet potatoes," Sam says, licking her lips.

"My Nana's recipe," I say.

"Dam girl. You slaving over the stove for that dick," Lisa says.

"Losing control for that dick," Sam says.

"Pulling up to the woods, following these hoes, for that dick," Simone says.

I feel my rhyming skills coming back. "Losing my mind for that dick, spending time on that dick, sending out these desperate bitch vibes, for that dick," I add.

We laugh.

"I think he was about to mate you," Sam says once we've settled down.

"What? When?" I ask.

"In the woods, but you were interrupted," Sam says.

"If that's true, why is he treating me this way now."

"I don't know. I'm sure he has some stupid, thought provoking reason," Sam says.

"I feel stupid. If I had listened, everything would be different. He told me. He told me to break up with Brian. He said we couldn't do anything until I did, but I was so in lust. I kept pushing, and I've been paying for it ever since."

"He's a really good guy. His feelings are hurt," Sam says.

"I see why you're trying to hold on to him," Simone says.

"She shouldn't have to try so hard," Lisa says.

"He's being a stubborn ass," I say.

"Then give up. Find somebody else," Sam says.

"I'm not giving up my mate," I say.

"That's the spirit," Simone says.

"Spoken by the woman who wanted to give up on hers," Sam says to Simone.

"Do I sense some drama?" I ask.

Simone's sweet demeanor changes. Her voice is deeper and faster. "My mate is a big baby who doesn't want to be a man and get married. I'm getting tired of his shit."

Sam and Lisa look stunned by Simone's outburst.

Sam speaks in a calm tone. "Simone, don't you love Wade?" she asks.

"Of course."

"Don't you know he loves you?" Sam asks.

"Sure."

"That's what matters, hon," Sam says. "Look, when Preston proposed, I wasn't expecting it or even thinking about it, but if he hadn't, I would've been happy just being his mate."

"Maybe for a little while," Lisa says.

170

"That's easy for you to say with your ring shining in my face," Simone says.

"Simone is feisty when she's mad at that boy," Lisa says, laughing.

"Simone, you have to remember Wade has been through a lot. He's not emotionally capable yet. It's a miracle he committed at all. You have to give him time and a little space," Sam says.

"I know you're right, but it's hard. I'm always walking on eggshells for him. Everybody else is getting married. What about me and what I want?" Simone asks.

"I hear you, sister," I say to Simone.

"You're stronger than him in that area. You have to be patient," Sam says.

"Girl, just sit back and enjoy yourself. Trust me, you don't want to rush it. That's the mistake I made. I fell too hard, too easily," Lisa says to Simone.

"Lisa, Michael has made up for what he did. Stop punishing him. He's a good man," Sam says.

Lisa rolls her eyes.

Sam turns to me. She places her hand on mine. "Shante, Jeremiah needs to deal with his feelings in his own way. What you've been doing isn't working. You're going to push him away. I know you don't want that, do you?"

"Of course not," I say.

"Now, the question is, what are we going to do about it?" Sam says.

"Is there anything we can do?" Simone says.

"Of course, there is? She's his mate. They're perfect for one another," Sam says.

"I'm having déjà vu," Lisa says.

"You and Michael are perfect for one another," Sam says.

"But it didn't come easy, did it?" Lisa asks.

"Most things worth having don't," Sam says.

"My mate came around when he got jealous, and when my life was in danger," Simone says.

———
171

"Possessive and protective," I say.

"The alphas usually are," Sam says.

"My Nana said I don't know how to handle an alpha."

"You don't, but that's why you have us," Lisa says.

"It sounds like you all have problems of your own," I say.

"But we've got our men," Lisa says.

She has a point.

"I'm running out of ideas. I don't know what else to do," I say.

"I think you're trying too hard," Simone says.

I hit the table. "I'm trying to fight for love, damnit," I say.

We all laugh.

"Preston did say throwing yourself at him is not the answer," Sam says.

"You need to do the opposite," Lisa says.

"Elaborate," I say.

"You're chasing him. He should be chasing you," Simone says.

"He's a predator," Sam says.

"Exactly," Lisa says.

"They say that about all men, but he's actually a predator. He loves the chase. He needs it," Sam says.

"If I leave everything up to him, nothing will happen."

"That's not true. You haven't allowed him to do anything. You're doing all the work for him," Simone says.

"We need to change your approach. When do you take his class?" Lisa asks.

"Mondays and Wednesdays."

"When you go to class tonight, you're going to act like nothing happened. Wednesday, you're going to be different, aloof, mysterious," Lisa says.

"I don't know if I can do that."

"You can. Just be nice. Instead of telling him, you want to make him wonder what you're thinking," Sam says.

172

"It's like a dance. Let him lead. And take your cues from him."

"You don't want to show him all your moves right away. You want him to reveal them over time, keep it exciting, keep him wanting more," Simone says.

"Let's practice," Lisa says.

"I'll be Jeremiah," Sam says.

"I wanted to be Jeremiah," Lisa says.

"You don't even know him," Sam says.

"This is crazy," I say.

"It'll be fun," Lisa says.

Sam clears her throat. "Hi, Shante," she says in her Jeremiah voice.

"I know you're not trying to speak to me after the way you treated me."

"Too much," Lisa says.

"I was joking," I say. "Hello, Jeremiah."

"How are you?"

"I'm fine. How are you?"

"I would say, fine. Thank you for asking," Simone says.

"Okay," I say. "Fine, thank you for asking."

"Don't try to pull him into conversation. Just walk away," Sam says.

"And you're sure this will work?" I ask the ladies.

"Yes," they all agree.

Sam clears her throat. "Is everything okay?" she asks as Jeremiah.

"Yes, why do you ask?"

"See how she jumps on any glimmer of hope," she says to the ladies.

They nod their heads and give me looks of pity.

"You don't need to know why he asks. You don't care," Sam says.

"You're unbothered," Lisa says.

"Don't seek his approval, and don't be grateful for his attention," Simone says.

"Is everything okay?" Sam asks again as Jeremiah.

173

"Everything's great," I say.

"Are you sure?" Sam asks.

I give her arm a friendly squeeze. "Jeremiah, everything's fine. I promise. My apologies, I mean, Professor Johnson." I give her a sweet smile, along with a shy look.

The ladies squeal with excitement.

"I have goosebumps," Simone says.

"Much better," Sam says.

"Let's talk about wardrobe," Lisa says. "Is this the kind of thing you normally wear to class?"

"Yes," I reply.

"You need to tone it down," Lisa says.

"You don't have to tempt him with short skirts and tight clothes," Simone says.

"He knows what's under there," Lisa says.

"You want him to use his imagination," Sam says.

"Wear something that accentuates your curves and covers them," Lisa says.

"You know Jeremiah. He might be drawn to a more classic look," Sam says.

They give me tips and a step by step plan. "I can do this," I say.

"You haven't heard the best part yet. You, my dear, are coming to the ball as my guest," Sam says.

"What ball?" I ask.

"The Alpha Ball. Preston is head of the Alliance Council, and I'm throwing the most extravagant party for the alphas. Jeremiah will be there, and you are going to walk into the room, you'll steal the show. Jeremiah won't be able to take his eyes off you," Sam says.

"That'll be perfect. We can give you a makeover," Simone says.

"I don't need a makeover."

"Nothing drastic. We'll enhance your natural beauty. I happen to be a makeup artist," Simone says.

"We'll get you a dress and do your hair, and you are going to snag that prince, Cinderella," Lisa says.

"I've never been to a ball before."

Lisa looks at her cellphone.

"No phones," Sam says.

"Sorry, Michael keeps texting me." Lisa stares at the screen. "Why does he keep sending me pics of motorcycles?"

"Jeremiah has a motorcycle," I say.

"This fool wants me to pose naked on a bike." Lisa shakes her head.

"You know you're going to do it," Sam says.

"I sure am."

We laugh.

"Okay, girls. I think Shante's good to go," Sam says.

Jeremiah's not going to know what hit him.

XVIII ~ Jeremiah

I'm in no mood to teach this evening, but I made a commitment, so I'll give it everything I've got. Any moment now, Shante's going to come walking through that door with her usual antics. She'll probably want to talk about what happened today. I've had time and drinks. I've calmed down, but I don't know what to do about Shante. I was trying to create a safe space for her, but maybe I've hurt her too much. Maybe she's better off without me.

Class begins in twenty minutes, and no one's here yet. As students trickle in, I politely nod and greet them.

"Good evening, Professor Johnson." I look to find Amber standing over my desk.

"Hello, Amber."

"There's something I want to talk to you about after class if that's okay."

"I'm available for all my students after class unless you want to talk now. There are still a few minutes before class starts."

"I think I'd rather wait until after."

"That'll be fine." Do I want to talk to Amber after class? No. I can scent what she wants, and it doesn't involve talking.

"Why do you need to talk to the professor, Amber?" Shante asks.

My heart skips a beat at the sound of her voice. I was beginning to wonder where she was.

"It's private. Amber flips her hair and walks to her seat."

"Good evening, Shante," I say.

"Good evening, professor. Hope you had a good day."

"It got a little rough around lunchtime, but I got myself together."

"Glad to hear it. We need you at your best," Shante says. She sits an apple on my desk. "This is for you. I got it from the grocery store." She's trying to piss me off, and it's working.

"Thanks." I take a bite.

She rolls her eyes and walks away. I tear my eyes away from her. There's no need to draw more attention to ourselves than necessary.

Other than the apple, Shante behaves the same as she has been in class. She's attentive. She answers all my questions at lightning speed. I'm turned on by how prepared she is. She and Amber trade a few quips, which is to be expected.

I'm relieved things seem to be normal.

Class is over, and I know Amber has been waiting. The students file out one by one. As I suspected, Shante and Amber are the only two students left. I'm kind of relieved Shante is here for once. I have no idea what Amber has planned. She sits patiently in the back of the class.

"Amber, you said you wanted to talk to me."

Shante gets out of her chair and walks out of the classroom. Where the fuck is she going? She would never leave me alone with Amber. Maybe she'll pretend like she forgot something and surprise Amber. But, she didn't leave anything behind. And, there's no trace of her scent. She's gone.

"I wanted to talk to you about extra credit or a little extra training maybe," Amber says.

"I don't offer extra credit." I gather my things and prepare to leave.

"I think I could benefit from it."

"Amber, you're one of my brightest students. You don't need extra credit."

"I was hoping for some real-world experience. I was wondering if I could shadow you for a day."

"No."

"But, Professor Johnson."

"I said, no."

"I thought I could get a better understanding."

"You can't just come to my job, Amber. What are you thinking?"

She looks like a deer in headlights. "I'm sorry."

"That's not how the real world works. Do you think I can allow strangers to walk into my office and go through my files? My job is serious. Information is privileged and sensitive, and you can't walk into the building and meet my boss or come to my office uninvited. You can't pop up when you feel like it."

"Professor, I never intended any of that. I'm sorry if I offended you."

I take a deep breath. "Shit, I'm sorry. It's not you." I stand.

Amber walks close to me. "Is it something I said?"

"No. It's been a long day."

She places a hand on my shoulder. "I understand. If you need to talk, I'm available. Would you like to go get some coffee?"

"I would, but I have a lot of work to do." I remove her hand from my shoulder. "Listen, next semester, you can take an internship. It's part of the program. I recommend you choose it as your elective. You have nothing to worry about. You'll fit right in at any law firm."

178

She grabs my hand and holds it between her palms. "Thank you, professor. I appreciate your time."

"I have to go. You have a goodnight." I walk out of the classroom. Shante has me losing my damn mind, and the one time I needed her interference in my life, she's nowhere to be found.

I'm fuming as I walk to my car.

Wednesday arrives. I must admit I'm curious to see Shante, and I can't help but look for her before class begins. Once again, she doesn't come early, as I thought she would. I check my watch. Class starts in one minute. I try to remain calm. I don't know if something happened to her or what.

I think I'm sweating. I tap my fingernails on the desk until I scent her. I feel like I can breathe because I know she's close. She walks into the room at six o'clock on the dot, and I have to do a double take. She's not wearing a short skirt today. She's wearing jeans and a button-down white shirt. One of the top buttons is undone, and I can't help but try to catch a glimpse of her perfect breasts. Her hair is pulled back in a ponytail that swishes from side to side when she moves. I want to grab that ponytail and pull it while she screams my name. My dick is instantly hard. I'm going to have to teach from behind my desk for a while.

"Glad you could join us, Miss Wilson," I say.

"Always a pleasure, Professor Johnson," she says with a smile. I don't know what kind of game she's playing.

I begin class. "Tonight, is going to be fun. Let's talk about torts. I trust everyone did the reading. Who can tell me what a tort is in their own words?"

I wait for Shante to speak up, but to my surprise, Amber answers. "Torts are cases where someone is injured and suing for damages."

"Correct," I say. Amber has a satisfied smile.

"And what are the three main types of torts?"

"Intentional, negligence, and strict liability," Amber says.

"Someone certainly is prepared," I say as I smile at Amber.

Amber looks pleased. I'm trying to figure out what's going on with Shante. She's not participating, but she's alert. She's watching. She's taking notes.

"Shante," I call her name.

She smiles at me. "Yes, Professor Johnson."

"What elements are required for a successful tort case?"

"Duty, breach of duty, causation, and injury." She does know the information, and she is paying attention. She seems fine.

"Torts covers a wide range and is the biggest category of civil litigation, so for the next couple of weeks, you will eat, breathe, and sleep torts. Everybody understand?"

"Yes, Professor Johnson," the class says in unison.

I continue with the lecture. Shante hardly looks at me. She doesn't flirt with me, and she doesn't even acknowledge Amber. I'm trying not to think about what's going on with her, but it's impossible to focus. Still, I get through class like the boss I am.

Once class is dismissed, I expect Shante to stick around, but she immediately gathers her books and walks away with everyone else.

"Shante, can I speak with you?"

She looks confused and stops in her tracks.

Once everyone is gone, I approach her. "Is everything okay?" I ask.

"Yes, everything's good. I enjoyed class today."

"You did? I'm surprised, because you barely said a word."

"I did. I've been waiting to get to torts."

I can't tell if she's being sarcastic or not. "Good," I say.

"Well, I'll see you next week." She walks away.

"Wait," I call after her.

She turns around.

"How are you holding up at the house?" I ask.

"I'm doing good. It was an adjustment at first, but I've gotten more comfortable. Thanks, by the way."

"No problem. If you need anything at all, call me."

"I will. Goodnight, Jeremiah." She touches my arm. "Sorry, I mean, Professor Johnson." She walks away.

I want to call after her again, but I resist. She says she's okay. I guess she's okay.

XIX ~ Shante

"Sam," I whisper into the phone.

"Hey, Shante," she says casually.

"He's here," I try to keep my voice low.

"Who's where? Are you in danger?" Sam asks.

"No."

"You scared me. Why are you talking like that? Who's there?"

"Jeremiah is here, at my house. Well, his house that I'm staying at. It doesn't matter. The point is, he's here. What am I supposed to do?"

"Stop freaking out. Why aren't you talking to him?"

"He's outside doing yard work or something. He hasn't come in."

"How long has he been there?"

"I don't know."

Sam laughs.

"It's not funny," I say.

"Get off the phone and get dressed. We're meeting the girls for brunch. I'll text you the address. Stay calm. You can handle this. Deep breaths," she whispers.

We hang up.

I take deep breaths. I can do this. I held it together this past week with encouragement from Sam, and I know it's a process. I haven't seen Jeremiah since Wednesday, and I haven't tried to contact him. I put on a powder blue maxi dress and twirl in the mirror. I'm not wearing any makeup, and I don't think I want to today. I put two goddess braids at the front of my hair and attach them in the back with a bobby pin. The rest of my hair flows in loose waves. I feel like a Grecian goddess.

I exhale, open the front door, and step outside.

Jeremiah stands. "Good morning, Shante." He's wearing sweatpants and a tank top. His body is glistening with sweat. My eyes bulge at his dick print. He looks delicious.

"Good morning."

"You look beautiful," he says.

I know I'm supposed to be cool, but I can't help but blush. "Thank you." I want to turn a cartwheel in the front yard.

He touches a lock of my hair. "I like your hair like this."

"Thanks. I thought I'd try something different today. I didn't expect to see you until Monday. What are you doing here?"

"I'm taking care of the yard."

"I would've thought you'd pay someone to do that."

"There's a project I wanted to take care of myself," he says.

"Looks like you've been working hard."

"I have. What do you think?" He points behind me.

I take my time turning around. I gasp when I see what he's working on. I want to gush and jump up and down. I want to jump in his arms and tell him how much I love it. I can't believe he did this for me. Is this a gesture?

"They're your favorites, right?" he asks.

"Yes." I turn to face him. "They're beautiful."

"I'm glad you like them."

183

I touch his arm, and my body responds. I want to jump on his dick, but I keep my cool. "Thank you, Jeremiah." I turn to look at the bold, colorful tulips once more before I leave.

"Where are you going?" he asks.

"I have some errands to run."

"What the fuck does that mean?"

"It means I have errands."

"Can they wait? I wanted to catch up with you, grab lunch, talk."

"I didn't know. I already have plans." I feel kind of guilty. He looks so sad, but I'm excited he wants to spend time with me. Of course, I can't let him know that.

"Well, Shante I—"

I cut him off. "I have to get going. I'll see you in class Monday."

"Sure," he says.

I head to the car, and he slowly goes back to the yard work. I need to get out of here now because I want him so bad, I'm going to burst.

When I arrive at the address Sam sent me, all the ladies are already there. I give them hugs and take a seat next to Simone. Everyone, but Sam, is drinking mimosas, and I help myself to one.

"You look amazing," Simone says.

"Thank you," I reply.

"I bet Jeremiah loves this look," Sam says.

I blush. "He told me I looked beautiful."

"I'm liking him more and more," Simone says.

"Look at that smile," Lisa says. "When you slow down and take your time, you get to enjoy these moments, these feelings."

"The butterflies," Sam says. "Do you feel the butterflies?"

"I do, but I'm freaking out."

"Why?" Sam asks.

"I think it might be working."

"Did you doubt us?" Lisa asks.

184

"A little bit, but now I'm questioning everything he says or does, every move he makes, and I'm questioning myself. I miss him, and it's hard not to talk to him or wait for him after class."

"It's temporary. You need to be patient," Simone says.

"Girls, Jeremiah showed up at her house today." She makes air quotes. "To do yard work."

"What?" Lisa laughs.

Simone and Sam laugh as well.

"Why is that so funny?" I ask.

"It's perfect. He wanted to see you," Sam says.

"I called you to ask for your advice, and you rushed me off the phone," I say to Sam.

"Jeremiah's a shifter. He can hear extremely well. I didn't want to risk him hearing our conversation."

"But it's working. He's making up excuses to see you," Simone squeals.

"You guys, I feel so bad. I didn't know what he was doing until right before I left. He was planting tulips in the front yard for me. He knows they're my favorites."

"So," Lisa says.

"He looked so sad."

"That's sweet, but it's not enough," Lisa says.

"He said he wanted to hang out or have lunch," I say.

"Not good enough," Lisa says.

"I thought it was sweet," I say.

"It is sweet, but the problem is these are minor efforts on his part. He expects you to be so grateful you'll accept his bad behavior. Don't forget, he constantly pushes you away," Lisa says.

"Lisa's angry, but she's right," Sam says. "Remember, no spontaneous plans, don't fall for meaningless gestures. And no matter what, don't sleep with him."

"I wouldn't call it meaningless," Simone says.

"Thank you, Simone. I don't think it's meaningless either," I say.

"Time for some tough love, Shante. This is going to be hard to hear. Are you ready?" Sam asks.

"No," I reply.

"Jeremiah showed up this morning and planted flowers for you. It's sweet, but he put down roots, metaphorically speaking, at a house neither of you calls home, and he has not made room for you in his actual home. Nothing he does makes up for that. He knows you're his fated mate. That's a huge deal. He's been waiting his whole life to find his mate, and you're in front of him, and he has not mated you. If he loves you, he should get your favorite flowers and bring them home, where he lives with you, his mate. Nothing less."

I take in everything Sam is saying. I bow my head.

Sam places her hand over mine. "Shante, you deserve so much more than being the girl he drops by to have sex with."

A tear falls from my eye, and I nod.

Simone reaches over to hug me. "She's right, you know."

I nod as I wrap my arms around her.

Lisa gets up and embraces us. "You're a catch, and you deserve to be loved. Really loved."

I hear sobs. Sam is in her chair, crying. "Sam, what's wrong?" I ask.

"Nothing."

"Are you in pain?" I ask.

"No."

"Why are you crying?" Lisa asks.

"It's my damn hormones." Sam attempts to get out of her chair. "This is so beautiful." She rubs her hand on her belly.

We make our way to her.

"Group hug," Simone says. We all embrace.

"You're a gem, Shante. I knew it the moment I saw you," Sam says.

I exhale and start singing. The first thing that comes to mind is, "thank you for being a friend. Travel down the road and back again."

186

All of the ladies join in with me. We really bring it home with the last line. We burst out laughing when we're done.

Applause erupts throughout the restaurant, and we take our bows before taking our seats.

"I get it. I really get it. I was going through the motions before, but now I'm not pretending anymore. I want to be the woman that wants more, that expects more. I expect to be treated like his mate, period."

"That's what I want to hear," Lisa says.

"And that is what you shall have," Sam says.

"I'll drink to that," Simone says.

"Thanks, ladies."

XX ~ Jeremiah

I can't believe I did that. I thought the tulips would impress Shante, but she barely said thank you. That was all I got for thinking about her and trying to do something nice for her ass. She's been acting strange lately. On Monday, she came to class and acted as if nothing happened. She didn't come early or stay behind. She didn't try to outdo Amber. She hasn't flirted with me or tried to get me alone.

I've gone out of my way to do better, but I'm not getting anything from her. As much as I'd hate to admit it, I miss her. I've been trying not to focus on her, but I want her. My body craves her touch. My hand wants to caress her. My lips miss her kisses. I can't wait to see her tonight.

Maybe tonight will be different. Class begins in twenty minutes, and there's a familiar scent approaching my door. It's not Shante.

"What the fuck do you want?"

"I can't come visit my son?" My father walks through the door.

"You and I have no more business," I say.

"I know."

"Then why are you here? I'm at work. My class will be here any minute."

"I need your help."

"With what?"

"The Alliance."

"I'm afraid I can't help you with The Alliance."

"I was given notice that The Alliance has revoked my membership."

"What does that have to do with me?"

"I've been a member of The Alliance for decades."

"You expect me to believe you're sentimental about that."

"I don't normally go out of my way to ask for favors, but I feel like you can help me with this."

"You have to know that I would never help you."

"Given the circumstances, I think the least you can do is get me a meeting with Preston Jacobs. He won't see me or respond to any of my messages."

"No. I'm not setting up a meeting with my boss, so you can attempt to trick him into thinking you're an upstanding citizen who's not going to use his organization to profit from illegal activity. I think I'll stay out of it."

"That's not what I'm doing, and this is important to me."

"Look, my understanding is Preston is making changes to The Alliance, and I have no influence there."

"I was going to let this go, but I heard they granted you membership."

"How do you know that?"

"Don't worry about how I know. You weren't a member before. What happened?"

"The only reason I wasn't a member was because of you, James. I didn't want to see you, but since I no longer care about avoiding you, I've accepted their offer to join."

"You took my spot," he yells.

"I did not. It has nothing to do with you."

"You don't want me to have anything. No respect. Nothing. You hate me so much that you want my name, our family name, to be worthless."

"Look, I want to be clear. I don't want to take anything from you, and I don't want to get involved in your business. I don't want you showing up in my forest or in my classroom. I have seen you more in the last week than I have in decades, and that's too much. I don't mix business with my personal life. If you want to a meeting with Preston, you need to get it on your own."

"You're right. I guess we're all on our own. Every man for himself."

"A man needs to be able to take care of himself. Isn't that right, James?"

"That's right, son. I guess I taught you well." He walks out the door.

Students file into the classroom. Shante, once again, doesn't show up early. At this point, I expect her to be here right on time. I don't want to have to put her out, but I'd have no choice.

I look at my watch. It's six o'clock. Shante's not here. If she's late, I'll let it go this once.

"Excuse me, Professor Johnson." I hear a faint voice. It gets louder. "Professor Johnson."

I lift my head. "Yes, Amber."

"It's past six."

"Thank you."

"You always start class right at six o'clock."

"I got it, Amber." I can't concentrate on class. Where the fuck is Shante? I clear my throat. "Tonight's assignment is going to be self-study. You have a project due next week. You may take the opportunity to go to the law library and prepare. I'll see you all next week."

The room is silent. "Goodnight," I say.

They slowly leave, but one student stays behind.

"What can I do for you, Amber?" I ask.

"Since class is out early, I was wondering if I could buy you a drink." She walks to the door and closes it before approaching my desk.

"Not tonight."

She moves to the side of my desk, inches away from me. "Maybe we can find something else to get into. I'm available for anything, anywhere, however you want it."

"What do you mean?"

"I mean, we can help one another relieve some stress."

"How would we do that?" I want to see how far she goes with this.

"I can think of many ways."

"That doesn't tell me anything. Go ahead and say what is is that you want to say." I can feel her nervous energy, and I don't feel bad at all. She started this.

"I'm saying I want you."

"How do you want me? Do you want me to fuck you on this desk?"

Her eyes widen.

"Don't get scared now," I say.

"I'm okay with that."

"I get rough. Do you think you can handle that?"

"I can take all that you've got."

I lean back in my chair. "Are you sure about this, Amber?"

"I'm sure."

"On your knees," I say.

"What?"

"On your knees. Right now."

She drops to her knees in front of my chair and runs her hands up my thighs.

I shake my head when she reaches for my zipper. "Did I tell you to touch me."

She quickly withdraws her hands. I can feel her nervous energy. Embarrassment is written all over her face. "Oh."

"Don't be scared, Amber. You see, I like to be in control. Do you have a problem with that?"

She shakes her head no.

"I asked you a question," I say.

She clears her throat. "No," she says.

"Get up," I say.

She stands slowly.

I take her hands, and she smiles.

"Amber, I'm not interested in you."

Her face turns red. "I thought—"

"Amber, you're intelligent and beautiful, and that behavior is beneath you. What did you hope to accomplish?"

"I like you. I just thought we could get to know each other better."

"You don't get to know someone on your knees. I'm your teacher. You're my student. You should be able to trust me not to take advantage of you."

"You wouldn't be taking advantage if we both wanted it."

"I would, and that's not fair to you. You should be spending your time with someone appropriate who appreciates the woman you are and all you have to offer, because you do have a lot to offer. You shouldn't be throwing yourself at someone like me."

"I'm sorry."

"You don't need to apologize."

"I should. I'm so embarrassed. Can we forget this happened?"

"Forget what?"

She tries to crack a smile. "Thanks, Professor Johnson."

"It's not a big deal."

"I must be crazy, thinking you'd be interested in me."

"It's not crazy. Maybe in another time, in another situation, things could've been different."

"And you're really nice. That just makes this harder."

"I'm not nice. You're not missing anything special here," I say.

"I'm going to get out of here. I'll see you next week."

"Goodnight, Amber."

"Goodnight," she walks away and turns when she reaches the door. "She's a lucky girl," she says.

"I don't know what you're talking about."

"She's a lucky girl." Amber walks off, leaving me with my thoughts.

I need to get out of here. Shante could be hurt or sick. I told her to call me if she needed anything. She hasn't called. She had to know I'd be worried about her.

I wrestle with whether or not I should call her. This feeling is one I'm unfamiliar with. I think I'm nervous, but I need to make sure she's okay. I'll check on her and hang up. My heart beats through my chest as I find her contact information.

The phone rings as I walk to my car.

"Hello," she says.

"Hello."

"Jeremiah, is that you?"

"Yes."

"What's going on? Is everything okay?"

"I was going to ask you that. You missed class tonight."

"Aren't you missing class right now?"

"We got out early."

"Since when do you let class out early?"

"If you had been there, you'd know I gave everyone the night to work on their projects."

"That's not on the syllabus."

"Things changed."

"You always follow the syllabus. Why did you change it?"

"I thought everyone could use the time to study."

"During class time?"

"Shante, stop questioning me about it."

"Fine."

I get into my car and drive. "Why weren't you in class?" I ask.

193

"I've had a long day. I got caught up, and I knew I wouldn't make it to class on time, so I decided to call it a night."

"Are you okay?"

"I'm fine."

"You had me worried. Could you at least tell me if you're not coming to class?"

"Do you require all your students to do that?" she asks.

"No, but you're not just any other student."

"I'm not."

"You know you're more than that."

"I don't know anything."

"So, are you okay?"

"I'm fine, Jeremiah. I'm just a little tired."

"Are you sick?"

"No, stop worrying. I promise, there's nothing wrong with me."

"Did you even think about me today?" I ask. I'm suddenly aware I sound like a female, but it's too late to take it back. The lack of contact with Shante has been making my life a living hell.

"Of course, I did. Why don't you tell me about your day? How was work?"

"I had to go to court."

"Did you win?"

"I was only arguing a motion?"

"Did you win?"

"Did you forget who you were talking to? Of course, I won."

"I would love to see you in action in the courtroom. I bet it's exciting."

"I get a rush out of it."

"I can imagine. Do you slam your hand on the table and yell, I object?"

I laugh. "Sometimes."

"That's passion. I can tell you love the law from watching you in class and from reading your book."

"Did you really read my book?"

"Of course, I did. I like this legal stuff too."

"I've noticed, or I did notice until about a week ago. You stopped participating in class. I hope I didn't cause you to lose interest."

"No, I've been giving the other students a chance."

"Is that what you've been doing?"

"Yes, Jeremiah."

"If you say so."

"Anyway, what inspired you to write your book?"

"I wanted people who feel like they don't have access to legal representation to at least have some basic understanding of the law and their rights."

"That's beautiful," she says.

"It's how I feel."

"I've been wondering something. You know what, never mind."

"What?"

"It's none of my business."

"It's fine. What is it?"

"With your resume, reputation, and knowledge, you could teach anywhere. Why do you teach at a community college?"

"I started out at community college. I had no money, and I was even homeless for a short time, but I was determined. Community college was there for me when I needed it, and there are a lot of people who are trying to make something of their lives. They live paycheck to paycheck, raise kids, work two jobs, all while trying to learn a trade or skill to give themselves and their families a better life. Those people need people with good resumes and reputations to give them quality information."

"I had no idea."

"People judge one another based on outside appearances, and that's to be expected, but I try to keep in mind, everyone has a story."

"I'm glad you chose to help people like me."

"I'm glad I'm able to. Also, if I didn't, I would've never met you."

"That's sweet of you to say. You're definitely full of surprises, Jeremiah."

"I hope that's a good thing."

"It is a good thing. Do you know this is the first time we've spoken over the phone?" she asks.

"Now that you mention it, I guess it is."

"This was nice."

"I agree. I guess I should call you more often."

"I wouldn't mind that."

"I'll make it happen."

"Okay." She sounds happy. "I guess I'll talk to you later. Goodnight, Jeremiah."

I'm wasn't ready to end our conversation. Why is she trying to get me off the phone? "Goodnight, Shante."

I'm a little pissed as I get out of my car and knock on the door. No answer. I knock again. Shante answers, wearing a t-shirt and short shorts. I swear she's more beautiful every time I see her.

"What are you doing here?" she asks.

"This is my house. I could've walked up in here with no warning."

"You will not come barging in here," she says.

"I didn't. Calm down."

Her arms are folded. She's sexy when she's angry. "Why did you come at all?"

"I called first," I joke.

She doesn't laugh. She only looks at me, expecting an answer.

"I wanted to see for myself you were okay."

"As you can see, I'm fine."

"You certainly are." I lick my lips.

"Are you flirting with me?" she asks.

"Does that bother you?"

"No, I like it."

"I'll have to do it more often."

"I look forward to it. Goodnight, Jeremiah."

"Can I at least get a hug before you throw me out?"

"You've never requested a hug before."

I pull her close to me. "I'm demanding one now."

"I like this side of you."

"Is that right?"

She wraps her arms around my neck. "Yes, Alpha."

I inhale the scent of fresh berries as I growl into her ear. "You know what that does to me."

"I know," she says holding me tight.

I place a soft kiss on her cheek. She turns her head, and my lips capture hers. Their softness electrifies me. I bite her tongue and suck as she presses her body closer to mine. It's been so long since I kissed her lips. I miss this feeling, this taste. My hand slips underneath her shirt. The warmth of her skin soothes me. My lips move to her neck.

She gasps. "Don't kiss me there," she says.

"Why not?"

"You know what that does to me."

"I know," I say as I kiss her collarbone.

"Jeremiah."

My hands are firm on her behind, and I rock her in my arms. It's a good feeling. We pull apart, but I want more. I need more. I lean my head in for another kiss.

"Goodnight, Jeremiah," she says.

I sigh. "Goodnight."

She releases herself from my hold and steps over the threshold. Have I lost her? Would I be okay if I lost her? Her body and her scent tell me she wants me, but she's not the same woman who was eager to have me.

"Wait," I say.

"Yes."

"What are you doing this weekend?"

"You'll have to be more specific."

"Saturday. What are you doing Saturday?"

"What time Saturday?"

"Eight o'clock."

"PM?"

"Yes, Shante. Eight PM."

"I'm going out with some girlfriends."

"Where are you all going?"

"I don't know. Wherever they want."

"What are you going out for?"

"That's a strange question, Jeremiah."

"Are you trying to meet someone?"

"What?"

"You heard me." My blood is boiling.

"No."

"Sure, you're not. You've been ignoring me, blowing me off, missing class. You know what, I get it. Don't even worry about it. I'm out of here."

"Jeremiah," Shante calls after me. "Stop. What's wrong with you?"

I ignore her as I get into my car and drive off. I am so done. I'm tired of bending over backward for her. She doesn't even appreciate it. I have options. I don't have to sit around waiting on Shante's ass to act right.

Someone is going to get this dick tonight, and I know just the person. Sarah lives five minutes from here, and she's always happy to see me.

I pull up to Sarah's house and ring the doorbell.

"Jeremiah, I wasn't expecting you." She tosses her shoulder length brown hair and bats her eyelashes at me. Her eyes turn green. She wants me.

I give her my sexiest stare. She bites her lip. "Would you like me to leave?" I ask.

"Don't you dare." She grabs me and pulls me into her house. I don't have to do too much to get Sarah. We know what this is, and we know what we do. She growls at me, and I growl back at her.

I grab her neck and push her back into the nearest wall.

"Tell Big Daddy what you want," I say.

"I want to please you, Alpha," she says. Sarah's an omega. An eager to please omega. She belongs to another pack, but she does whatever I ask, without talking back.

That's exactly what I need. She touches my cheek, and I flinch. "You're upset," she says. "What can I do?"

I don't want to talk. I kiss her.

She runs her hand across the front of my pants, unzips them, and strokes my dick.

"Tell me what you need," she says.

I reach underneath her silk lingerie and touch her skin. "To fuck," I reply.

"That would be my pleasure."

I lift her against the wall.

She wraps her legs around my waist. "I'm glad you stopped by, Handsome."

I smile.

She covers my face with kisses.

It feels good to be wanted. I kiss her chest, making my way down her breasts. Why can't everything be this easy.

"Ummm," she moans.

"You know what I need," I say.

"What?"

"A little appreciation. How about that?"

"I can do that." She kisses my neck.

"Would it be too much to acknowledge that I'm trying? Is that too much to ask?"

"No. Kiss me." She presses her lips to mine.

I pull back and put her down. "I'm making a fucking effort, and I get nothing." I pace back and forth across Sarah's plush carpet. "I planted her a garden, and she doesn't show up. And, I canceled my class for her, all for her. She barely reacts. I was trying to be thoughtful. Fuck."

"Jeremiah, I'm not sure—"

"What the fuck is wrong with her?"

"Jeremiah," she yells.

"Ungrateful."

"Jeremiah," she shouts.

"What?" I yell.

"Have you told her?"

"What?"

Sarah is frustrated with me. She walks over and smacks me upside my head. "Tell her how you feel. Stop trying to make her guess what you're thinking, and tell her already."

"I was being romantic. Shit."

"And I bet she's still trying to figure out what all that means. You have to make your intentions clear. Show her the alpha that you are. Do you understand?"

"Yes.

We stand in silence.

"I—" I'm trying to find the words to say to Sarah.

"So you're in love," she says.

I nod.

"Well, get the hell out of my house, wasting my damn time. You got me wet and horny as fuck while you're crying about some other chick."

"I'm sorry."

She rolls her eye and I feel like shit. Then she smiles. "She'd better be worth it, Jeremiah. You certainly are."

I kiss Sarah on the cheek. "She is." I zip my pants and leave.

It takes me less than five minutes to get back to Shante. I pound on the door.

"I'm coming," she says. She opens the door. She opens her mouth to talk, but I don't give her the chance.

"Listen to me. I was trying to ask your ass out on a date, and you don't even care. That's fucked up. I canceled class for you because you weren't there, and I come over here to check on you, and you don't even care."

"I do care."

"I'm not done. I wanted to take you somewhere nice on Saturday, but you have to go out with the girls. That's fucked up, but it's fine. I'm taking you out on Sunday. I'm not asking, so if you have plans, cancel them. You have plans with me now. I'll pick you up here at seven. Wear something nice." I pull her in for the best kiss of her fucking life.

When I'm done, she's breathless. Desperate for more.

"Goodnight," I say, and I walk off with a satisfied smile on my face.

When I get into the car, Shante is still standing in the doorway, watching me. I sit in the car until she goes inside and locks the door.

I hear her say something before I drive off. One word. Butterflies.

XXI ~ Shante

"Shante, you look so beautiful. Jeremiah is going to be speechless when he sees," Simone says.

I look at myself in the mirror. My eye makeup is usually black and heavy. Simone gave me a smoky eye with deep earth tones. It looks more natural but still stands out. My lips are a barely-there pink color. Luscious curls are pinned to one side, hanging below my shoulder. "Simone, you did a beautiful job. Thank you."

"You're welcome." She gives me a hug.

"I'm so nervous."

"Don't be. You look amazing. Jeremiah won't be the only one staring at you."

"I don't even know what I'm expecting."

"You're expecting to have a good time. That's all. There will be great food and drinks, and we will all be there for support. We're going to have a good time."

"I don't want to be the seventh wheel."

"You won't be. Sam and Preston will be busy schmoozing all night, so you'll be the fifth wheel," Simone says.

"That makes me feel much better. Thanks, Simone."

"Okay, here is your dress. Your car will be here in an hour. I have to go make sure Wade is dressed like an adult."

"I'm sure he is."

"You'd be surprised. He has an unlimited supply of tight ass t-shirts, but when he puts on a tux, he makes my knees weak."

"Doesn't he always make your knees weak?"

"He does."

"I can't wait to see Jeremiah in a tux. He's the only man that looks sexy in a sweater vest."

"I can't wait to meet him," Simone says.

"I'll see you there," I say. I walk Simone out and lock the door.

There's a something special that I want to wear tonight. My grandmother gave it to me for my twenty-first birthday. If the ladies are right, this will be a night to remember. I feel like she should be with me. I know she's in heaven rooting for Jeremiah and me. I open my jewelry box and pull out the floating diamond necklace. I never had anywhere special to wear it, and it's perfect for tonight.

The time has come for me to put on the dress. I trusted Sam to pick it out, and I have no idea what it looks like. What if it doesn't fit? What if I hate it? I pace before I finally unzip the garment bag.

"Wow, it's gorgeous." I touch the fabric. The sapphire dress is encrusted with jewels and has a plunging neckline. It's fitted at the waist and hugs my curves perfectly, flowing to the floor with a slit up to the thigh. It's perfect. I've never had anything so beautiful. Sam is my fairy godmother. How did she do this?

The doorbell rings while I'm trying to attach my necklace.

"Sorry, I thought I had a little more time," I say as I open the door.

"You look beautiful."

I lift my head. "Strike? What are you doing here? Jeremiah is not going to like this." I look around.

"You look beautiful," he says.

"You already said that."

"It's true," Strike says.

"Thank you. You need to leave."

"Where are you going?"

"Out with some friends."

"Not with my brother?"

"Strike, I'm not going to listen to your assessment of my relationship with your brother. You need to stay out of it."

"You don't have a relationship with Jeremiah. But, you could have a relationship with me."

"No, I can't."

"Shante," he touches my cheek.

I flinch. "Don't."

"I'm so sorry."

"You need to leave."

"Don't push me away."

"Strike, you need to listen to me. I love Jeremiah. Only Jeremiah. And I believe in him. I'm sorry. I can't give you what you want."

Strike pounds his fist against the doorframe, causing me to jump.

"Hey," a voice yells from behind Strike. I've seen this guy before. He was at Jeremiah's party. *Jonathan?*

Strike turns around.

"Is there a problem here?" Jonathan asks.

"No. This gentleman was just leaving." I turn to Strike. "Goodbye, Strike."

Strike pauses a moment before he walks away.

"Are you okay?"

"I'm fine, Jonathan. What are you doing here?"

"I live next door."

"I haven't seen you this whole time."

"I'm a busy man. I'm not home a lot."

"Did Jeremiah ask you to watch me?"

"Listen, if you ever need anything, just let me know. You really do look lovely," he says before he turns away.

I go back inside and finish getting ready. I don't know how Sam found shoes to match this dress or how she knew my size, but my look is complete. The doorbell rings at eight o'clock on the dot.

"Good evening, Miss Wilson," the driver says.

"Good evening."

"My name is Anthony. I'll be driving you this evening. Are you ready?"

"I guess so." I grab my purse and lock the door.

"Don't be nervous. You look beautiful," he says as he holds the door open for me.

Anthony asks me a few questions, but I can't concentrate. I'd normally participate in small talk, but all I can think about is the ball. He gets the hint, and we ride the rest of the way in silence.

"We're here," he says.

I'm a little bummed that I'll be walking into the room alone.

The street is bustling with town cars, limousines, and valets running around in a frenzy. Couples walk towards the building in their finest. I'm giddy and nervous, but there's a line to drive to the front of the building, so I have some time to pull myself together.

When we finally get there, Anthony opens my door and takes my hand. "Have a good night, Miss Wilson."

"Thank you, Anthony."

People stare as I walk up the steps. I give my name to the woman working the door, and she allows me entry. The hallway is crowded. I hope to see a familiar face, but nothing yet. A man opens the ballroom doors, and I step inside. It's spectacular. Music plays as couples dance. There are countless elegant tables with expensive linens and centerpieces of red roses, the reddest roses I've ever seen. There are three giant wolf sculptures carved out of ice.

A waiter walks by with a tray of champagne. I gladly take one to calm my nerves. The place is buzzing with people, but I haven't spotted any of the girls yet.

"Dance with me." I hear a voice in my ear.

I turn around. There's a muscular man with blue eyes and long brown hair staring at me. I gulp down my champagne.

He takes my glass and sits it on a nearby table. "Let's go." He extends his hand.

I don't think saying no is an option. I nod because I find it hard to speak. He's definitely good-looking.

He takes my hand and leads me to the dance floor.

I place a hand on his shoulder and the other in his hand. He places his hand on my waist.

"I'm not used to this type of music," I say.

"Neither am I. I just wanted to be close to you."

Well, damn. "Aren't you forward."

"Did you come here alone?" he asks.

"I was invited by a friend."

"Where is your friend?"

"I don't know yet. I just got here I was looking around for her."

"And instead, you found me. Do you have a name?" he asks.

"Shante."

"Shante, forgive me for being forward. I don't hesitate when I see something I want."

"I don't know if I should be flattered or offended. Do you have a name?"

"Cornelius," he says.

"Cornelius, I am not a *something* for you to possess. I'm a woman. I have my own will. I have ideas. And I make my own decisions. Do you understand that?"

"I think I'm in love," Cornelius says.

I laugh. "I don't think you can handle a girl like me."

"Give me one night, and I'll change your mind." He dips me.

I have to catch my breath. "I'm not going to lie, that was sexy."

He growls. "Let's get out of here." His blue eyes turn green. I know what that means.

"No, thank you."

"I'm not taking no for an answer."

"You are tonight." I take my hand off his shoulder. "Thank you for the dance." I try to walk away, but he squeezes my other hand and pulls me closer.

"I'm not letting you get away, Shante."

"Please, let me go."

"Give me a chance, and I promise you'll never say those words to me again."

"I'm trying to be nice," I say.

"She's being nice, but if you don't let her go, I'm going to rip out your throat."

I turn around, and Jeremiah is there, looking sexy as sin in a black tuxedo. "Jeremiah," I say.

"This is none of your concern," Cornelius says.

"I'm not going to tell you again," Jeremiah says.

"I saw her first. She's mine," Cornelius says.

"I'm not yours," I say to Cornelius.

"Quiet," Cornelius says.

"Excuse me," I say. "Let go of my damn hand."

People are starting to stare. I don't want to cause a scene at Sam's party.

"Shante is mine. You don't want to challenge me on that," Jeremiah says.

Cornelius loosens his grip on me and steps toward Jeremiah.

I pull my hand away. "Shante belongs to Shante," I say as I back away.

"Walk away," Jeremiah says to Cornelius.

"Make me."

Jeremiah grabs Cornelius by the throat, lifts him in the air, slams him into the ground, and places his foot on Cornelius' neck.

Four men in black suits rush to pull them apart.

"Shante, there you are." Sam, Lisa, and Simone walk toward me.

I'm relieved to see them. "I'm so sorry," I say. "I wasn't trying to cause a scene."

"It's not your fault," Sam says.

"I know how important tonight is. I didn't mean for this to happen."

"Girl, look around. This place is packed with testosterone. I'd be worried if there wasn't an incident."

I look around for Jeremiah. I don't see him or Cornelius.

"They're going to cool off for a moment," Sam says.

"Look at you starting fights. I want to be like you when I grow up," Lisa says.

"You look gorgeous," Simone squeals.

"I knew this dress was perfect for you," Sam says.

I give each of the ladies a hug.

"You look good, queen," Lisa says.

"You guys," I blush. "Please continue."

They laugh.

"Hey," I say.

"What's up?" Sam asks.

"There are some sexy ass men behind you. Who do they belong to?" I recognize Preston, but the other two I have yet to meet.

The men walk over to where we're standing.

"Good evening, Shante. It's good to see you again." Preston pulls me in for a hug.

"Nice to see you as well," I say.

"That's enough," Sam says.

I raise my hands.

"I was just being nice to your friend," Preston says. He wraps his arms around Sam.

"Shante, this is my boyfriend, Wade," Simone says.

"Really, Simone? I'm your fucking mate. You'd better quit playing with me," Wade says.

My eyes widen. That damn Wade has some fire in him, and he's sexy as hell.

———

208

"Simone is just joking," I say. "It's nice to meet you, Wade."

"My mate," Simone says. She looks in his eyes and smiles. He kisses her.

"I love you," he says. I can tell he loves her, and all she wants is to be married to him.

Wade gives me a hug. "Shante, right?" Wade asks.

"Yes," I say.

"I recognize you from the picture," Wade says.

"What picture?"

"The one on Sweater Vest's phone."

"Sweater Vest?" I ask.

"What's the matter with you?" The other gentleman says. This one has a sexy beard, a handsome face, and a nice body. He must be Lisa's mate.

"Shante, this is my mate, Michael," Lisa says.

Michael gives me a hug.

"Nice to meet you," I say.

"The pleasure's all mine."

"What picture?" I ask.

"He has pictures of you on his phone," Wade says.

"Maybe he didn't want you to tell her that," Preston says.

"Well, she knows now," Michael says.

"How do you know that?" I ask Wade.

"I saw them," Wade says, "one of you and him and one of you on a motorcycle."

"We took those the first day we met," I say.

Sam squeals.

"Sam, calm down," Preston says.

"I knew it," Sam says.

"Hey, you need to be worried about this man right here," Preston points at himself.

"Somebody needs some attention," Sam says. She turns around and wraps her arms around Preston's neck. He adjusts his body to make room for her belly. They look like the perfect couple. She's wearing a satin black dress

209

and a red rose pinned to it, and he's in a black tux with satin lapels and he has the same rose pinned to his jacket.

Simone is staring at Wade like she's going to rip his tux off and Lisa and Michael are holding hands.

"I knew I was going to be the seventh wheel," I say.

"Preston," an older man interrupts Sam and Preston. They turn to greet him and are pulled into conversation.

"See, you're the fifth wheel," Simone laughs.

I chuckle. "Much better. I need a drink."

"I got you one."

I know that voice. Everyone looks behind me. They all have goofy grins on their faces.

My heart skips a beat. I'm scared to turn around. I place my hand on my stomach and try to take deep breaths.

I can feel the warmth of his body, and I can smell him.

"You're beautiful," he says.

"You think so?"

"Absolutely breathtaking." He hands me a glass of champagne.

He can't see my face, but I know I have the biggest grin. I look at my friends. Sam gives me a thumbs up.

A finger grazes my arm. I shiver at his touch. "Jeremiah," I say.

He growls in my ear. "I missed you," he says.

I sip my drink. He presses his body against mine. I can feel how much he missed me.

"What were you doing? Dancing with him?" Jeremiah asks.

"I was only being polite."

"I don't want you dancing with anyone else."

"I didn't know that. I thought you needed time."

"I meant what I said. You're mine, and the only man you're going to dance with is me. You remember what it's like to dance with me?"

He puts his arm around my waist.

"I remember everything you put me through, and I meant what I said. I belong to me."

"Let me be clear, Shante, you belong to me, and I belong to you. There will be no more misunderstandings. No more games. I am your alpha."

I'm speechless.

"Who's your alpha?" he asks.

"Jeremiah B. Johnson, JD," I say.

"That's what I'm talking about," Sam shouts.

I turn around to face him and bite my bottom lip as he rests his hands on my hips.

"I thought you were going out with the girls tonight," she says.

"I was, but they ditched me for these guys." I point behind me.

"I wanted to have you on my arm tonight. You were supposed to be here with me."

"I didn't know that."

"Now, you do. And now you're mine."

Jeremiah grabs my hand and walks with me to the group. "Good evening," he says.

Everyone says good evening.

"You must be Simone." He kisses her hand. "Wade didn't do you justice. He doesn't deserve such a beautiful mate."

Simone blushes. "Wow, I love him," she says to me.

"What the hell are you smiling at?" Wade asks Simone.

Jeremiah steps in front of Lisa. "You must be Lisa. I see why Michael is so in love with you. You're a beautiful woman."

"Thank you," Lisa gushes.

Wade extends his hand.

Michael growls.

Wade shakes Lisa's hand with a smile.

"Samantha, it's always a pleasure," Jeremiah says. He extends his hand.

Preston steps between Sam and Jeremiah.

"Really, Preston?" Sam says.

Jeremiah shakes Preston's hand. "You didn't even warn me," he says.

"I didn't know she was coming until tonight."

Jeremiah looks at me. "Who do I have to thank for bringing you here?"

"My girls," I say.

"Thank you, ladies, I've got it from here."

"She's special," Lisa says.

"Be nice to her," Simone says.

"I will treat her the way my mate should be treated," Jeremiah says.

"She's not your mate," Sam says with her arms folded.

"She will be tonight," Jeremiah says.

I think I just hallucinated. The ladies gather around me, congratulating and hugging me.

"What?" I ask.

"Tonight," Jeremiah says.

"Are you ready for this?" Sam asks.

"Hell, yeah," I say.

Jeremiah grabs my hands. "I want to apologize for mistreating you. I should've never pushed you away. I should've never resisted you, and I'm going to make it up to you. Do you forgive me, baby?"

"Yes, yes. She does," Simone says.

"I'll think about it," I say.

Jeremiah kisses my lips.

"What's gotten into you?" I ask.

"I need you," he says. He takes my hand and leads me to the dance floor.

"I know you're not ditching us for a man," Lisa says.

"Sorry," I shrug.

Lisa winks.

Jeremiah's strong arms pull me in as the music swells.

"I don't know how to dance to this."

"Follow my lead," he says. He places one of my hands on his shoulder and the other in his hand. "Stand straight, shoulders back. Let my body guide yours. You know how to do that, don't you?"

"You tell me," I blush.

"You're very good at that," he says.

His grasp of my body is strong, but I concentrate on mirroring his movements. When moves his leg forward, I move mine back. He moves his leg to the side, and I do the same.

"I had no idea you could dance like this," I say.

"This is nothing. Get ready." He releases my arm and pushes me out. I spin and hold my free hand out as he holds his hand out. I'm in awe. He tugs my hand, and I spin back into his arms. He lifts me off the floor and twirls me around. I gasp from the rush. He stares into my eyes and places me on my feet. I know this look, and as much as he wants me, I want him more.

I'm led into a series of twirls, spins, and lifts. I hold on and go with the flow. I feel like I've jumped off a bridge, and I'm falling. It's a calm rush. I want to be in this moment forever.

The music comes to an end, and Jeremiah places me on my feet.

Applause erupts around us.

"Kiss me, my mate," I say.

He gives me a tender kiss as another song plays. We're wrapped in one another's arms, and our bodies sway from side to side.

"I love you," he says when we pull away.

"This feels like a dream."

"Imagine my surprise when I scented you in the room. Then I saw you. I know I'm late, but I've been trying to change. I had to put my pride aside and show you how much you mean to me."

"That's a nice speech Jeremiah, but how do I know you're not going to flip out on me again?"

"I confessed my love and apologized in front of all our friends. What more do you need?"

"I need to know what happens next."

"We go home, we mate, and we live our lives."

"How do we live our lives?" I ask.

"Together."

"Are you going to come visit me at your investment property? Or my apartment?"

"Are you out of your fucking mind?"

"Jeremiah," I shout. He couldn't last five minutes without flipping out.

"You're coming home with me, to our house and our bed, woman. You're not living anywhere but with me. Forever. And if you think otherwise, you're mistaken."

I hit his chest. "Why didn't you just say that?"

"I didn't think I had to."

"I hope this is real."

"I promise you it's real."

"Are you sure it's me you love and not the dress and the makeup? I'm not polished or quiet. I'm not sophisticated like the women you're used to."

"Shante, this," he touches my gown, "is a beautiful gown, but it's just a dress. You can change your hair and makeup. You can sit quietly in the front row of class. You can say what you think I want to hear, but those things don't matter. I fell in love with the woman who stormed into my class and challenged me when I tried to put her out. You were quite the opponent."

"So were you."

"I fell in love with the woman who refused to go home because she promised to visit her Nana and the woman who got me to open up about things I haven't talked about my entire adult life. I know who you are, and that's who I fell in love with. Shante Wilson, damnit."

I laugh.

"I'm sorry it took me a while to get here. I was such an idiot. I could've lost you," he says.

"It wasn't all your fault."

"I was stubborn way longer than I needed to be."

"You were quite an asshole," I say.

"Thankfully, you put up a good fight," he says.

"You're worth it," I say.

His eyes change colors. "Let's get out of here. Now."

_____

214

"Can you spin me one more time?"

"Whatever you want."

"I love you, Jeremiah," I say as he spins me out.

This is the happiest moment of my life.

XXII ~ Jeremiah

The roads are mostly clear. I'm driving a little over the speed limit. I can't wait to get Shante out of that dress and into my bed.

Shante sits next to me dancing to the music she's playing on the radio. I smile as she starts singing badly at the top of her lungs. I couldn't be happier.

We come to a red light at an intersection. I stop the car thinking in five minutes I'll have her at home. I get to take her and claim her.

The light turns green and I take off. I have a smile on my face as I breeze through the next intersection.

"You're in a hurry," she says.

"I don't know what you're talking about."

"You can't wait to get to all of this." She runs her hands down her body."

"Something like that."

She laughs at me as we reach another intersection. The light is red. I come to a stop, and it turns green almost immediately. As I take off, I turn to smile at her and I see headlights headed towards my car at dangerously high speeds. It's a big eighteen-wheeler. My reflexes are fast, but there's no way to avoid a collision. This truck is coming straight at me. I step on the gas, but the truck is inches away from my car, inches away from Shante.

"Shante!" I yell. I reach for her. Everything happens so fast, she doesn't have time to react. The look of terror in her eyes as the truck collides with my car is imprinted in my memory. The sound is a horror that I will never forget. I get a glimpse of the driver. It's my father. My brother sits in the passenger seat.

My car is pushed through the guardrail, and flips over and over as we roll down. I feel every bang, every flip.

I feel Shante's terror and hear her screams as the car crashes, bangs, and rolls. It feels like forever until we stop.

Everything goes quiet.

I gasp for air as I come to. I have a headache. I'm a little disoriented. I try to focus my eyes and remember what happened.

The car is upside down and my body feels contorted. It's hard to breathe. I look around.

Shante lies in the seat next to me. I can smell her blood. I don't know how badly she's injured. I need to get up. I need to get to her. I rip my seatbelt off and reach for her. My shoulder is dislocated. I wince as I pop it back into place. I take deep breaths as it heals.

"Shante, baby, can you hear me?"

She groans.

I rip her seatbelt. She lies upside down with her eyes closed. "Shante, stay with me," I beg.

I lift my door handle and push. The door is stuck. I push against it with all my strength until it swings open. "Shante, I'm going to get you out of here."

I run to her side of the car and rip the passenger door off. Tears are in her eyes. There's a gash on her head. Blood streams down the side of her face. I don't know the extent of her injuries, so I carefully pull her out and away from the car. I am terrified. Her heartbeat is weak and her breathing is shallow. She's bloody and bruised. I'm pretty sure she has a broken arm.

"Shante, you're going to be okay. I'm going to get you out of here."

She's unresponsive.

"Fuck," I yell.

I hear voices in the distance. They're heading our way.

"What did you do?" William asks.

"You'd better decide right now where your loyalty lies. He betrayed us." It's my father.

"So you tried to kill your own son? He was right about you."

"Stop acting like a little girl. He took something from me. He disrespected me. I won't tolerate that."

"You hurt Shante, you bastard. I'll kill you."

I rise to my feet. I see my father approaching. "You!" I shout pointing at the man that should've loved and nurtured me. Rage builds within me. My father walks toward me with his arms wide open and a smirk on his face. "I'll be right back," I say to Shante.

She groans, but I can't let this go.

His pack is nearby. I hear footsteps approaching from a distance, and I can scent them. He planned this. He planned this ambush.

"Why?" I shout as I walk toward him.

"Shante," William shouts. He runs to her side. I let him go, because my focus is on my father right now.

"You betrayed me for a piece of ass." He shouts at William. "You and your brother. There's nothing special about this girl. What's wrong with you two. She's a problem, a distraction. I got lucky that she was in the car with you."

I remove my shoes. "I did nothing to you. All I ever wanted was to be rid of you." I take off my jacket and unbutton my shirt. "You couldn't just leave me the fuck alone."

"The Alliance turned on me and threw a party. The Head Alphas want to humiliate me, and you, my own son, helped them.

I remove my pants.

218

He continues. "No one gets away with that. I'm taking over, and you can join me and take over my legacy, or you can be my enemy. I'm not asking anymore, son."

"You chose for me, old man."

I growl, baring my canines to my father as I shift. My father shifts, as well. This motherfucker is going to die today, and no one's going to stop me from ripping his head off. I use my hind legs to lunge with more fury than I've ever experienced. My father jumps, and we collide. He sinks his claws into my back, and I aim for his sides. I dig both hands in and tear. I can smell his blood, but it's not enough.

We trade hits, blow for blow. He's always been skilled and feared, especially by me, but I'm not a child anymore. He almost killed me when I was just a boy, and I told myself that day he'd never do it again.

I growl, thinking about the pain he caused me and the hell he must've put my mother through. He scratches me across the face. I rise to my hind legs and do a backflip. *I'm not the boy you beat all those years ago.* Unfortunately, because he's my father, I can speak to him through our mind link. I recover on all fours and charge him. I bite his neck and dig my claws into his stomach.

He whimpers and claws at my skin. He's still a powerful beast, but he's injured. He struggles to grasp a hold of me. I bite his neck again and bring him to his back. I shove my claws into his stomach before he can move. Blood gushes from his insides. I jump on top of him and claw into his body. I think about all the blows I took as a child and unleash all the rage I've been holding on to. I claw at him for every hit, for every punch, for every kick.

I shift back into my human form. "You're no alpha," I say. "You never were."

He howls and whimpers from the pain.

"Shift," I shout.

His wolf obeys. "I'm the fucking alpha," I shout. My father lies before me bloody and beaten.

"I'm your father," he says between coughs and blood spewing from his mouth. "Have mercy."

"Men don't show mercy," I say.

William stands next to our father.

"Strike, stop him."

"You hurt Shante," he shouts.

"Idiot." He coughs up blood.

Strike turns his back to our father.

"It's over, James," I say. I fall to my knees and extend my claws. "Ahhhh," I yell as I sink into the side of his neck as deep as I can with my palm facing his face.

He screams, bringing all other activity in the room to a halt.

I puncture him in the same manner on the other side, then I go for the jugular. I hold my hand and pull, channeling all my rage. My mind is consumed with images of Shante bleeding and unconscious. I feel his neck snap, and it's satisfying. I feel his skin tearing. I'm not stopping until his head is completely detached. His eyes are horrified and wide open. That's how I will remember my father as I rip his head from what's left of his neck.

I stand waving his head in the air as I howl. His pack has closed in. All eyes are on me. Two of them growl as they approach me.

I walk toward them. "Are you sure you want to do this? I'll have both your heads."

They slowly retreat.

"Bloodbond Pack," I shout. "Your alpha is dead. I am your alpha now. Bow to your alpha."

The wolves of his pack bow and howl. "Shift," I shout.

Their wolves obey their alpha.

"Things are about to change. Anyone who has a problem with me come forward now. What I say goes. Does anyone have a problem with that?"

No one speaks.

I wave the head again. "I asked a question," I shout.

"No, Alpha."

"You all belong to me. Nobody make a fucking move until I tell you to do so or you answer to me. I won't tolerate the slightest whiff of insubordination. Do I make myself clear?"

"Yes, Alpha."

"Get the fuck out of here," I shout.

They move slowly.

"Now," I shout. I throw the head into the darkness.

"Jeremiah, I'm sorry. I didn't know." My brother walks over to me.

"I need you to keep them in line for now. Can you do that?"

"Yes."

"Look at me William."

He looks in my eyes.

"I'm only giving you one chance. Do you understand me?"

"Yes, Alpha," he says.

"If you fuck this up or fuck me over, I will kill you. Our last fight was nothing. I can torture you and keep you in excruciating pain, let you heal, and do it all over again. There will be no more chances. Understood?"

"Yes, Alpha."

"What I said goes for you too. Nobody makes a fucking move without my approval. Somebody tries something, they die. Understood?"

"Yes, Alpha."

"Get the fuck out of here, and call an ambulance."

"What about Shante?"

"Death is coming for her, and you and your father are to blame. She's my mate. I'll take care of her. Get out of here before I kill you too."

I run to Shante and gently rest her head in my lap. I'm filled with sorrow and regret.

"You can't leave me, baby," I rock back and forth. "We're supposed to be together. We're supposed to mate, and you have to get your degree, remember? We're supposed to have babies. Three boys and two girls that look just like you. You have to fight. Fight to stay with me. I'm so sorry. I was stupid. I wasted all those months, but you can't leave me, Shante. I can't live without you. Please." Tears stream from my eyes. I feel so helpless. I bend over and kiss her lips. The tears won't stop flowing. I sob uncontrollably. "You're the only woman I've ever loved, the only woman I'll ever love. Please, don't leave me." Her heart rate is slower and slower. We've reached the end. I can't believe this is happening. I hold her face close to mine. "I'm so sorry Shante. You only wanted to be with me, and if you die, you're going to die as my mate. Come to me, my mate," I say. I sink my teeth into her lower neck. I feel a pulse, a burst of pure energy. I feel connected to her on every level.

"*I love you, my mate,*" I hear her voice through my mind link before the connection fades.

"No," I cry out. "Don't leave me."

XXIII ~ Shante

My eyes shoot open and I gasp for air. I remember dancing. I remember being happy, and everything faded. I'm standing, surrounded by darkness. I don't know where I am or how I got here. A mirror appears before me. I'm staring at myself dressed in all white, but it's not a reflection. It's me, but it's not me.

"Am I dead?" I ask.

"Not quite," she replies.

I turn around. I'm staring at myself, the me that was in the mirror in all white. Peace and happiness radiate from her.

"Who are you?"

"I'm you, Shante."

"Where am I?"

"You have to decide, lil' girl."

"What do you mean?"

She says nothing.

"Tell me what to do," I say.

She fades away. Her body turns to dust and is carried away by a gust of wind. A white wolf appears where she stood. At first, the wolf has my eyes, but then they turn green.

I feel a connection with the wolf. She knows my thoughts. She feels my pain. She's me.

I jump when I hear Jeremiah's voice. He's crying, calling my name, begging for another chance. I feel his anguish, his guilt, and his love.

"I'm here, Jeremiah," I say. "I'm here." But he can't hear me. I feel like I'm talking into a void. "What do I do?" I say. "Jeremiah," I shout.

The white wolf howls and walks toward me. Jeremiah's wolf appears by her side.

"Jeremiah," I shout.

His wolf looks at my wolf.

"Jeremiah, I'm here. I love you," I shout.

His wolf nuzzles my wolf.

"I choose you, Jeremiah. If I get to decide. If I have a choice, I choose you," I shout.

The wolves run together, heading straight for me. It happens too fast for me to react. I brace myself to get knocked over. Their bodies appear to be one as they jump into me.

"BITE!"

I gasp for air.

"Shante," Jeremiah yells.

My teeth extend into canines and I lunge forward and attach myself to Jeremiah's neck.

There's a flood of energy before everything turns black again. When I come to, my body is in agony. It hurts like hell. I feel like I'm falling, like I'm going to crash and nothing can save me. My bones bend and snap. I want to cry, but instead, a howl comes out of my mouth. I jump to my feet and look down. I don't have feet, I have paws. I'm covered in white fur. It's the wolf. She's me. I lift my paw and study it. What happened to me? Where am I?

I look up and see Jeremiah staring at me. I take a step back. I growl. Jeremiah walks toward me. I growl again. I don't know what's going on.

I hear Jeremiah's voice in my head. *"Shante, it's okay."*

"What's happening? What's happening? I say in my head.

"Do you know where you are?"

"I remember being at The Alpha Ball."

"We were in a car accident. Do you remember?"

It all comes flooding back to me. Jeremiah reaching for me as I look over and see bright headlights heading right for us.

"You're okay, now."

"Is this a dream? Did I die?"

"No, you came back to me."

"What happened to me?"

"You shifted. You're a beautiful white wolf."

"How?"

"We're mated."

He walks to me.

"Stay there," I say. I take a step back.

He stops moving and shifts in front of my eyes. *"You're like me,"* he says. *"I need you to come to me, please, baby."*

"I'm scared."

"Don't be. I won't let anything happen to you again. Come to me, my mate."

I cautiously make my way to him. He rubs his head against my neck, nuzzling me. His touch awakens me. I howl.

"Shante, shift. Shift for me so I can hold you in my arms."

"What do I do?"

"All you have to do is see it, and it'll happen."

I close my eyes and picture myself standing next to Jeremiah, and my body transforms.

"Jeremiah," I say. He's holding me so tight. "That hurts," I say.

"Sorry," he says. He pulls back and looks at my body. He touches and pokes me.

"What are you doing?" I ask.

225

"Making sure you're okay. Your wounds have healed."

I touch my side, no pain, no bleeding, no scar. It's as if nothing happened.

"It was my father," Jeremiah says. "He did this."

"Really."

"I'm sorry, Shante. It was my job to keep you safe."

"It's not your fault. I should've let you kill him the first time. I just didn't want you to have to do that. Did he get away?"

"No, I ripped his head off. He'll never hurt you or anyone again."

I nod.

Jeremiah puts his jacket over my shoulders and puts his clothes on as I sit.

I can hear sirens.

"You need to get checked out," Jeremiah says. "I need to get rid of my father's body." He grabs his father's body and head and take off running. He's back minutes later.

Voices approach. "Hello, is anybody down there? Hello."

Jeremiah shouts. "We're down here," until someone reaches us.

The ambulance checks us out, and the police ask us what happened. People keep telling us how lucky we are to survive a crash like that without any injuries. Jeremiah tells them it was a hit and run, and we don't know who the driver was. Once we get the all clear, a cop drives us home.

Other than occasionally asking if I'm okay, the ride is silent. I can't talk because I don't know what to say or how to feel. Jeremiah is worried. I can feel it, but now is not the time for me to deal with that.

When we arrive at his main house, our home, he carries me. I notice something is different. It's been a long time since I've seen this place, but I swear those tulips weren't here before. My heart swells. I tug at him, and he

226

puts me down. I walk to the bed of flowers and run my hands over them.

"I planted those for you," he says. "I know they're your favorites."

Jeremiah is thoughtful and caring. He gives me a bath and puts me to bed. "Get some rest," he says.

Sleep is difficult, but when I'm finally able to keep my eyes closed, I sleep for an entire day.

When I open my eyes, there are balloons and flowers all around me. There are gift baskets and food baskets. I have no idea where all of this came from. I find a card on one of the baskets. It's from Sam and Preston. There's also some things from Simone and Lisa.

I venture into the house and follow Jeremiah's scent. He's in an office. When he sees me, he rises to his feet. I make my way to him, and he captures me in an embrace. I exhale. I'm comforted by the warmth of his skin and the connection my soul feels to his. I remember the times I opened my eyes and he was sitting next to me, watching over me. I can feel his love for me.

"Let's get you something to eat," he says.

I nod.

"Your friends brought plenty of food. Do you want some lasagna?"

I nod.

He holds my hand as we walk to the kitchen. We eat together in silence. When I'm done, I just want to go to sleep. I give him a kiss on the cheek and walk upstairs alone.

I awaken the next morning to a huge breakfast. Jeremiah takes my hand and leads me to the kitchen.

I hear his voice in my head. "*I love you, Shante.*"

The last thing I want is for him to think that I don't love him.

"*I need to know that you're okay. Are you able to talk?*"

I nod my head, yes. I'm pretty sure I can talk. I haven't really tried. I'm just emotionally exhausted. He's been so patient and understanding. I walk to his chair and sit in his lap, giving him a tight embrace. I do love him, and I want to feel close to him. I kiss his lips. He's hesitant before he kisses me back. He lays his head on my chest and holds me. This feels good. I want more of this. Something awakens in me. My body heats, and I remove my robe. He kisses down my neck and my breasts. He pushes his plate out of the way and sits me on top of the table. I kiss his chest and unbutton his pants. He lies me down. His desire is as great as mine. I feel what he's feeling. I was told to expect that after mating. I prepare myself for his invasion. I can't wait to feel him inside me, but the invasion never comes.

"You're not ready," he says.

I place my hand between my legs and put my finger in his mouth so he can taste how ready I am. His eyes change colors.

"No," he says.

Instead of protesting, I hop off the table. I go up the stairs to our bed and close my eyes.

"Lil' girl, what's wrong with you?"

"Nana? Is that you?"

She sits next to me on the bed. She looks younger. Her skin is fresh and glowing, like when I was a little girl. It looks like she's never known sickness or death. "I know who I am. Do you know who you are?"

"Yes, ma'am."

"I can't tell."

"I don't know if you've noticed, but I've been through a lot."

"I noticed, but you also gained a lot. You have good friends, a good mate, and you're a shifter. I always wanted to be a shifter."

"It's a bit much."

"I know, child, but you are strong enough to handle all of it. Don't you know that?"

I shrug.

"You are, baby. Didn't Nana tell you to always use your voice?"

"Yes, ma'am."

"Who are you?" she asks.

I smile.

"I asked you a question, lil' girl."

"Nana."

"Don't make me get a switch. Who are you?"

I shout. "I'm Shante Wilson, damnit, and you'd better not forget it."

Nana brushes my cheek with her finger.

"Damn right," she says.

She holds me close and rocks me from side to side. "I miss you, Nana."

I squeeze her before she fades away in my arms.

I wake up in a cold sweat looking around the dark room. It was all a dream. I smile to myself. Nana is right. "Thanks, Nana," I say.

Today is different. I feel like a new woman. Jeremiah is still asleep, so I go to the kitchen and make him breakfast. I guess the food hits his nose because I hear him moving around before he comes downstairs.

"Good morning," I say as he stands in front of me.

"Shante," he rushes to me, picks me up, and spins me around.

"Can I get this level of excitement every time you see me?"

"You can have anything you want from me."

"Anything?"

"Just please don't stop talking to me again."

"I promise you, I won't."

"I missed your voice annoying the hell out of me."

"Well, you are going to get an earful over the next couple of days. We have so much to catch up on. I haven't said a word in days. You're going to get tired of me."

"I could never get tired of you. I'm just relieved that you're back. I thought I was going to have to take you to a psychiatrist."

229

"I was overwhelmed, not crazy."

"You scared me. I thought you were gone."

"No matter how bad things get, I'll always come back to you, Jeremiah. I love you."

"I love you, too."

"Sit down," I say.

He sits as I prepare his plate. "How do you feel?" he asks.

"I feel really good now. I had to remind myself that I had a life to get back to."

"You would've never gone through any of this if it weren't for me. I don't want you to suffer because of me."

"Don't say that."

He takes my hands in his. "Listen, you can get out of this. I know this isn't what you signed up for. If you need to be free of this life, you can go and never look back. I'm sorry, Shante." He hangs his head.

"Jeremiah, look at me," I say. "Don't you ever say that shit to me again."

"I was just—"

"I was never under the impression that being with you would be easy. We've had ups and downs, but I wouldn't trade any of it. I was meant to be your mate, and that's what I want to be. Let's move forward and focus on our future, not the past."

"I'm glad to hear you say that."

XXIV ~ Jeremiah

I thought I had broken her. I thought I had saved her, only to lose everything I loved about her. She didn't talk for five days. For five days she didn't communicate with me, only head nods, some of the time.

Those were the worst five days of my life. I felt helpless. I didn't want to push her. I could only pray that she came to herself again. It's been a week since she started talking. We slowly got into a routine and back to our daily lives, working and living together. We both returned to school, and she resumed being my star student. Life is good.

After a long day at the office, I can't wait to get home and see my mate.

As I approach the door, I hear soft music playing. I wonder what Shante's doing in there. I drop my briefcase when I step into the foyer. There are candles all over the room, and my eyes find Shante behind the flickering of the flames.

"Good evening, Alpha," Shante says.

"What's going on here?"

"I'm sad to say that I'm very disappointed in you."

"What did I do?"

"You haven't done anything, Alpha. I can't remember the last time you touched me."

"Shante, quit playing."

"I'm not playing." She steps in front of the candles, completely naked.

I lick my lips. "That's not fair."

"What's not fair is how you've neglected me."

"I would never neglect you."

"You have, and I want to know why. I want to know right now."

"I just want to make sure you're okay. You've been through a lot. We have plenty of time to connect. We don't have to do anything you're not ready for."

"How many times do I have to tell you I'm fine. You don't have to worry about me anymore."

"I have to be sure."

"I'm not going to break, Jeremiah. See for yourself." She takes my hands and places them on her breasts.

I feel her heartbeat, and it's hard to fight the urge to squeeze. I desperately want her, but I'm hesitant.

"You don't want me anymore?" she asks.

I place her hand in front of my pants. "Feel that. I always want you, every time I see you or think about you since the moment we met. I just don't want to move too fast."

"Then let's take it slow." She leads me to the kitchen. There's chocolate sauce, ice, honey, and fruit on the table.

"What is this?"

"Have a seat." Shante takes a pineapple slice dipped in chocolate and feeds it to me.

"Ummm," the pineapple juice bursts in my mouth and meets the sweet taste of the chocolate. "That's good," I say.

She straddles me in my chair, and I can't fight the desire to touch and squeeze her body. "Can I have a kiss?" she asks.

"You may."

___

232

She sticks out her tongue and squeezes chocolate sauce on the tip before she kisses my neck, causing my body to tingle. She loosens my shirt buttons and kisses my lips. There's still a faint taste of chocolate on her tongue, and I'm going to savor every drop.

She whispers in my ear. "I've got something else you can taste."

I inhale and sink my fingers into her ass, kneading and pulling her into me. She grabs a bottle of honey and drizzles it down her neck and chest. My mouth waters with anticipation of licking and sucking it off her.

"Take your time," she says.

I begin at the center of her neck. She rolls her head back as I suck. I swirl the honey onto my tongue and then explore her mouth. She removes my jacket.

There's still more honey for me to taste. She growls when I grab her hair and pull her head back. I can no longer fight the craving I've had for her since we mated. I lick the honey from her chest and bite her nipple, then I suck. The more she moans, the harder I latch on. I squeeze her breasts together and take turns putting them in my mouth while she grinds against my hardened dick.

I can smell her desire, and I can feel how much she wants me. I've been fighting it for a week now, but I'm not fighting it anymore, and she's not going to let me fight it.

She undoes another button from my shirt and then decides to rip it off. I'm aroused by the sound of the fabric ripping and buttons falling to the floor. She drizzles chocolate on my neck and chest and licks and sucks it all off.

"Okay, I think you're ready," I say.

"I've been ready," she says.

"I've been waiting."

"Fuck me, Alpha, and don't hold back."

I pick her up and sit her on top of the table. "Open."

She opens her legs wide for me, and I lick my lips. I lay her down and pour the honey between her legs and watch as it runs down her lips, into her pussy. I unzip my pants and stroke my dick. I can't wait to lick every drop. I take the chocolate and drizzle it over the honey before I dive in, spreading the syrup with my tongue, devouring her pussy, savoring every moan that comes from her mouth. I grab a piece of ice and press it against her clit. She cries out. Her hips lift off the table. Her body writhes against my mouth, and she presses my head down.

I'm lost in her scent, in the taste of her essence mixed with the sweet taste of chocolate and honey. Once the ice melts, I suck her clit. She circles her hips until she cries out. Her body shakes, and she moans her delight. I insert my finger in her tight pussy, moving in and out while she comes.

I like to watch her with her mouth wide open as she tries to catch her breath.

"Damn, Jeremiah."

I continue to kiss down her thighs, making small bites along the way. I pick up the chocolate sauce and drizzle it over her toes. I start with the pinky toe and work my way up to the big toe, taking them into my mouth and sucking as I massage her foot.

"Oh," she says. She's caught off guard at first, but she enjoys it by the time I move to her other foot. She moans as I apply pressure to her arches and play with her toes with my tongue. She squeals when I suck. Once her body is relaxed and ready, she gets down from the table and turns her back to me, lowering herself onto my dick, slowly.

"Fuuuck." I unbuckle my pants, and my eyes roll back into my head. This pussy is so wet and tight. I missed the feeling of our bodies connecting. I grab her breasts and squeeze, holding on to her as tight as I can. It'll probably bruise, but it feels so good as she slowly circles her hips. The warmth of her magic electrifies every cell in my body. I bite her back every time she moans. "Ride this dick," I whisper.

"You like that?" she asks.

"You feel so fucking good."

She really sinks down. My hands guide her hips. I groan in pleasure. She was definitely made for me, and now I need to show her what this alpha dick does.

Without warning, I bend her over the table, pressing my hand into the small of her back. I slam my body into hers, and she cries out, screaming my name as I take her.

"Fuck me, Alpha." This woman knows what I like to hear.

I grab her hair and pull. She likes that shit. Her hips meet mine thrust for thrust. The table is rocking. Fruit is falling, but I don't give a damn. She starts to scream, and her pussy clenches my dick. I hold on to her as she comes, timing my rhythm with her breathing.

I remove my clothes and turn her around to face me. "When we mated, we didn't get to have the whole experience, and I want it now. Is that okay with you?"

She nods.

"Let me hear you say it."

"Yes."

I carry her to the living room where she has a blanket lying on the floor and place her on top of it. I take my time entering her, kissing her lips, making love to my mate who I need. Warmth overtakes me. Her moans echo in my ear. She digs her nails into my back, gripping me with passion, meeting my hips with intensity. I'm close, and so is she. I bite her ear as I release into her, my body depleting. Everything I have pours into my mate. I bite her neck, she bites mine. Pleasure I've never known courses through my body, and we become one. Our connection is sealed. We're both spent. That's the last thing I remember before drifting off to sleep.

I wake up in the morning feeling like a new man. My mind is clear, and my bond with Shante is solid.

She stretches and yawns.

"Good morning," I say.

"Good morning."

"How do you feel?"

"Like I'm ready to run a marathon."

"I know what you mean."

"What do you want to do today?" she asks.

"Let's work off some energy," I reply.

"How?"

"Why don't we go to the forest?"

"Why don't we go shopping?"

"Shopping?"

"Yes, we can get you a new sweater."

"You got jokes."

"No. I love your sweaters. You can never have too many."

"While we're there, we can get you another short ass skirt, or do you already have them all?"

"What?" She jumps on top of me growling. "You're going to pay for that."

I flip her over and pin her to the floor.

She gasps.

"I love you."

"I love you too."

"We're mated," I say.

"I know," she says.

"We should celebrate."

"What do you people usually do?"

"You're my first mate, so I don't know."

"I'd better be your last mate."

"How about you'll be my only mate?"

"Perfect."

He kisses me on the cheek.

"This is a big deal for you. What would you like to do?" she asks.

"There is one thing, but I don't think you'll be up for it."

"Try me."

XXV ~ Shante

The next thing I know, we're on Jeremiah's motorcycle, pulling up to Blue Ridge Forest.

We walk through a familiar path. It looks a lot different in the light of day.

"Can I ask you something?" I ask

"Sure."

"How's Strike doing?"

"He's fine."

"You have to make sure he's ok. He's your brother."

"I'm looking after him. He's keeping an eye on my father's old pack while I take care of you."

"You know I only love you," I say.

"I know."

"I just wanted to check on him."

"I know."

"After the accident, I remember hearing him praying for me."

"Really?" Jeremiah asks.

I nod.

"Well, I'll have to thank him for that."

"Please do."

"I'm not as worried about him, now that my father's out of the picture, after what he did to you."

"You still need to keep him on a short leash."

"I know. Trust me. I told him if he wants more responsibility, he'll have to show me that he's willing to learn and change."

"That'll be good for him. He looks up to you."

"I seriously doubt that."

"I don't."

Jeremiah takes a deep breath. "How does it feel to be out here?" he asks changing the subject.

"I'm not as scared as I was the first time I was here."

"You mean when you were sneaking around?"

"I had to keep my eyes on you. Why did you want to come here so bad?"

"This place is important to me. We're home. Blue Ridge Forest is our territory. I'm alpha of the Blue Ridge Pack, and as my mate, this is your home too."

"I don't know where I would fit in with the pack. They don't know me like they know you."

"They'll respect you as my mate, and together we'll run this pack."

"We will? Don't tell me you messed around and gave me some authority."

"You think you can handle that?" he asks.

"I can."

"It's important for the well-being of the pack that you are a part of our family. You can take on as much or as little as you want."

"Let's take it slow and build from there," I say.

"No problem."

"Thank you."

"Did you bring me all the way out here to give me that speech?"

"I wanted to see how you felt here."

"I feel good. Now we can go shopping."

"Your wolf should be connected to this place. Can you sense her?" he asks ignoring my request.

"Yes."

"She is a part of you. You need to embrace that. You need to listen to her, and trust her instincts."

I nod.

"What's wrong, Shante?"

"Nothing."

"I can feel it. My wolf can sense when you're uneasy. I need you to talk to me."

"I don't know if I can live my life that way. What if I didn't do it again?"

"Do what?"

"Shift."

"Why wouldn't you be able to do it again?"

"I don't know. It happened so fast. It was scary, and it was painful."

"It's like that the first time, but it gets much easier."

"I don't know. What if I just don't shift? Will you still love me?"

"I'll always love you. It's not like we shift all the time, but it's not something I want you to be afraid of."

"It's easy for you to say. You've been doing it your whole life."

"Not my whole life. I was a teen when my first shift happened."

"But it's easy for you."

"And it will be for you too. You can't be afraid, and I don't want to push you, but we have to get you comfortable. This is part of your life now, and you need to accept all parts of yourself. Wolves can smell fear, and we have a new pack that answers to us. Our family is about to get larger, and they need to respect you and me."

"I don't know."

"You know how when you're a kid and you were learning how to ride a bike."

"Sure. I don't know what that has to do with this."

"Remember the first time you fell."

"Yes."

"If I know Nana, she didn't let you give up after that. You had to get right back on the bike and try again."

"Right."

"That's what I need you to do. I can't let you stay on the ground. If you live your life in fear, it'll swallow you, and the Shante I fell in love with is a brave, shit-talking, trouble maker."

"Damn right."

"I need you to own it. You need to understand how this works. Tell me who's your alpha."

"Really?"

His expression turns serious. "When I tell you to do something, you do it. My pack calls me Alpha. Do you know why?"

"No."

"That's who I am. It's my responsibility to lead and protect. You have to understand that when an alpha tells you to do something, you do it, and you don't talk back. Who's your alpha, Shante?"

"You're my alpha. Am I expected to bow now?"

"You're expected to take this seriously."

"Okay."

"Now, Princess, you are going to get back on that fucking bike. Do you understand me?"

"Okay." I can feel the wolf within stirring. She's determined. She hangs on to Jeremiah's words. I think she's waiting on his command.

"Fear is not an option, and you will not disappoint your alpha. Do you understand?"

"Yes." He was so nice a few minutes ago.

"Yes, what?"

"Yes, Alpha."

"You'd better be sure because if I get a whiff of fear from you, you'll be punished. Do you know what happens to scary ass, weak ass wolves?"

"No."

"They're tormented, mocked, shamed, and placed at the bottom of the pack. They're not respected, and they're not pitied. My mate will not be a weak ass wolf. You're strong and smart. I'm going to give you one shot to get this right because I'm not fucking around. If you want to be with me, you have to be able to survive."

I think I know what's coming. "Yes, Alpha."

Take off your clothes.

I do as he says.

"Picture yourself as that beautiful white wolf and shift. Now."

I know I can't hesitate, and I have to push past the fear. Neither myself nor this wolf wants to disappoint Jeremiah, so I close my eyes and concentrate on the wolf I saw in my dream. She runs toward me and jumps into my body, and I begin to transform. Jeremiah was right. It doesn't hurt so much this time. It's still very strange how my bones reshape, and suddenly, I have fur.

My wolf howls when my shift is complete. Jeremiah howls back. I look up and am surprised to see that he's shifted too. I look at my paws and my white fur. This shit is crazy.

I'm startled when I hear his voice in my head.

Good job.

Thank you, Alpha. How are you in my head?

We can communicate this way.

I'm going to have fun with this, I reply.

How do you feel?

Strong.

That's good. You need to hold on to that. You're a powerful beast. Your body will change, and I'm sure you noticed all your senses are magnified. You'll have to get used to the strength that you have now.

Okay.

Walk around. Make sure you can use your body.

It's weird to be on four legs instead of two. I take my time walking around the field, stretching my legs, and feeling the energy of my wolf.

Jeremiah should take it easy on me, but he doesn't. He pushes me to use my body to run and jump and my voice to growl, bark, and howl. He wants me to get comfortable. He knows what he's doing. I can tell he's a good alpha. He must've known that if he didn't push me, I wasn't going to do shit about this wolf.

Finally, when the sun sets, he gives me a break.

"Was that supposed to be a celebration?" I ask.

"Didn't you have fun?" he asks.

"Hell no."

He holds my hand as we lay in the grass, staring at the moon.

"What does our future look like again?" I ask.

"You'll get your degree. We'll get married. We'll have five kids, three boys and two girls."

"I changed my mind," I say.

He sits up. "About what?"

"School. I don't want to be a paralegal."

"What? Why not?"

"I don't think it's right for me."

"You were doing great. You have a knack for this. You can't give up."

"It's my decision to make."

"It's the wrong decision. You need to think about this."

"I have. I don't just want an associate's degree anymore. I want to get my bachelor's degree and then go to law school."

"Don't play with me, Shante."

"I'm serious. You don't think I can do it?"

"Of course, I think you can do it. You can wear down any opponent."

"So, you're okay with it."

"I love it. I just have one stipulation."

"I'll hear it, counselor."

"We should get you knocked up right now."

"Now?"

"We'll have a baby or two while you work on your associates and your bachelors. Then you can concentrate on law school."

———

"I object," I say.

"Do you really?" he asks.

"No, I'm just practicing."

"So, you want to."

"I do. I can't wait to have little alpha babies."

"And I can't wait to make you my wife."

"What did you just say?"

"I want you to be my wife, now."

"Don't play with me, Jeremiah?"

"Have you ever known me to joke around?"

"No."

"I'm serious. Do you want to get married, or not?"

"Yes, I want to get married. I didn't wear you down for nothing."

"I know a judge that can do it, or we can go to Vegas."

"Let's go to Vegas," I say.

"Let's go." He stands and grabs my hand.

"Right now?" I ask.

"Yes."

"I like this spontaneous side of you."

He kisses me, and we both howl at the moon.

"I would've loved to be there."

I'm all smiles as I sit on the bed in our luxurious hotel suite.

"Everything happened so fast, my head is still spinning. The next thing I know, we were on a private jet," I say to Sam over a video call. All the girls are with her as I share our news.

"I'm so excited for you guys," Sam says.

"We all are," Lisa says.

"Thank you," I say. "We went to the jewelry store and he got me this big ass rock for everything he put me through."

"I never said that," Jeremiah says.

"You deserve it," Sam says.

I have to admit, I'm a little worried about Simone's reaction. I know she really wants to get married, and I notice she's quiet.

"Yeah, you're a married woman. Congratulations," Simone says. I hear the strain in her voice.

"Thank you." My heart goes out to her, but I don't want to make her feel bad so I don't say anything else.

"Show us the ring again," Sam says.

"I mean, that's just tacky," I say as I use my hand to emphasize my point, making sure my ring is front and center in the camera. "I'm not going to be one of those women who uses any excuse she can to flash her ring," I say as I wave my hand. "I just won't do it."

"It's gorgeous," Sam says.

"What was the wedding like?"

"It was cute, in a little chapel. Jeremiah cried."

"I did not," he says.

"It's okay for men to cry," I say.

"I don't do that," he says.

I laugh. "I'm tripping. He was masculine the whole time. He didn't even crack a smile."

"Much better," he says.

The girls all laugh.

"How does it feel to be mated and married," Sam asks.

"I'm happier than I've ever felt in my entire life. I feel like I'm going to burst."

"We are so happy for you."

"Thank you ladies, for everything."

"We didn't do anything," Lisa says.

"You guys became my friends. I feel like you're the sisters I never had."

"We love you Shante," Simone says.

"Yes, we do," Sam says.

"Me too, Lisa says."

"I love you girls too." I feel compelled to break into our song. "Thank you for being a friend…"

We all sing together.

Jeremiah looks at me like we've lost our minds. He shakes his head. "I hate to break up the fun, but Mrs. Johnson has some wifely duties to attend to."

"Hi, Jeremiah," they all say.

"Bye, ladies. We'll see you soon."

"Bye," they say in unison.

I wave before I end the call.

"You do realize marriage is a legally binding contract," I say to Jeremiah.

"Of course, I know that. It's the most important contract of my life, and I meant what I said. I'll love you, protect you, and honor you forever," he says.

My wolf presses against my skin. I feel my eyes shift. "Kiss me, my mate."

Would you like to keep up with Zoe Ray? Follow Zoe on social media for updates.

Website
http://www.sincerelyzoeray.com

BookBub
https://www.bookbub.com/profile/zoe-ray

Goodreads
https://www.goodreads.com/author/show/14773767.Zoe_Ray

Facebook
http://www.facebook.com/sincerelyzoeray

Instagram
http://www.instagram.com/sincerelyzoeray

Twitter
http://www.twitter.com/sincerelyzoeray

Other titles by Zoe Ray
Some of your favorite characters from Alpha Professor can be found in these stories:

Alpha Boss
Mark Of The Dragon

Alliance

My Night With Preston (One Night Stand Series Book 1)

Teach Me: My Night With Wade (One Night Stand Series Book 2)

Bundles

The Alpha Boss Collection (4 book bundle)

On Fire For Wade (2 book bundle) (Teach Me and Mark Of The Dragon)

Romantic Suspense
He's Mine Not Hers

www.ingramcontent.com/pod-product-compliance
Lightning Source LLC
Chambersburg PA
CBHW011940260626
47157CB00018B/3265

9 781735 918419